Black Fx Literary

M A G A Z I N E

Issue 27 Cover Art: *Tropical Forest* by Sarah Jane Walker

ISBN: 978-1-959787-05-1

Editors' Note

Here we meet again, this time within Issue #27! Last month we celebrated THIRTEEN years of *Black Fox Lit*! What a joy it is to bring together the talented voices that fill these pages. We believe that each piece in our summer issue feels like a conversation—a unique exchange between writer and reader.

As you read through the issue, you'll find stories that feel like they're crafted just for you, poems that hold emotions you might have thought were yours alone, and essays that make you see the world a little differently. Our contributors have put their entire hearts into their work, and we think you'll feel that connection as you read. Whether you read the summer issue by the pool, in the shade of a leafy tree, or on a park bench, our hope is that you find something in these pages that makes you pause, reflect, imagine, and maybe even smile.

One of the reasons we work so hard to keep *Black Fox* alive is because of the literary community. There are still so many stories to tell, and we want to help bring them into the world. As always, thank you to our contributors, team, readers, and supporters for being here. Thank you all for helping *Black Fox* continue to grow. We know we say it all the time, but our magazine is made possible because of our phenomenal lit community. Expressing our immense gratitude never gets old. Here's to another issue filled with words that matter and inspire.

We are truly yours,

~ The Editors
Racquel and Elizabeth

Meet the BFLM Staff

Editor in Chief:

Racquel Henry is a Trinidadian writer, editor, and writing coach with an MFA from Fairleigh Dickinson University. She also owns the writing studio, Writer's Atelier, based in Orlando, FL. Racquel has been a featured author, presenter, and moderator at writing conferences and MFA residencies across the US. She is the author of the novellas, *Holiday on Park, Letter to Santa, Christmas in Cardwick, Meet Me in December, The Write Gym Workbook*, and *The Writer's Atelier Little Book of Writing Affirmations*. Her fiction, poetry, and nonfiction have appeared in various literary magazines and anthologies. When she's not working, you can find her watching Hallmark Christmas movies.

Managing Editor:

Elizabeth Sheets is a writer and an editorial associate for the Research Development office at Arizona State University. She earned an MA in Narrative Studies from ASU. Some of her favorite authors are Patrick Taylor, Stephen King, Anne Rice, Fredrik Backman, Kristen Arnett, and Sarah Waters. Elizabeth's fiction, nonfiction, and poetry appear in *Kalliope – A Consortium of New Voices, Black Fox Literary Magazine, Mulberry Fork Review,* and *Apeiron Review.*

Poetry Editor:

Heather Lang-Cassera is a full-time lecturer with Nevada State College, a Tolsun Books publisher, a *300 Days of Sun* Faculty Advisor, and a Clark County, Nevada Poet Laureate Emeritus. She was a 2022 Nevada Arts Council Literary Arts Fellow. She is the author of *Gathering Broken Light* (Unsolicited Press, 2021), which was written with the support of a Nevada Arts Council grant and won the NYC Big Book Award in Poetry, Social/Political. Her next collection of poems, a book of ecopoems with the working title of *Firefall*, has been acquired by Unsolicited Press for publication in 2025.

Readers:

Cassandra Brown is an avid reader and hobbyist writer based in Denver. She holds a degree in English Literature, enriching her discerning eye for compelling narratives and poetic expressions. As a poet herself, she understands the intricacies of the creative process and the courage it takes to put one's work into the world. Cassandra's depth is not limited to literature; she is also an accomplished software engineering leader and a mother of two. You can find her on Instagram @apixelatedpoet.

Rachel Gonzalez is a writer from Goodyear, Arizona. She holds a BA in English with certificates in Creative Writing and Literature, and will be finishing her MA in English Literature this winter. She is the acting writer-in-residence for The Fictional Cafe. An avid hiker and rock climber, she never leaves the house without a book or a pen. Some of her favorite authors are John Green, Becky Chambers, Fredrik Backman, Forrest Leo, Isabel Allende, TJ Klune, Cherrie Moraga, and JRR Tolkien.

Arniecea Johnson is an emerging fiction writer in Chicago, IL. She has an MFA in fiction from Columbia College Chicago and has been a Fiction Judge for the annual Young Authors Writing Competition. Her short stories have been published in *Masks* and *Kansas City Voices*. When she's not writing or reading, Arniecea enjoys visiting aesthetically pleasing brunch spots and watching horror films, good or bad.

Liana Johnson is a writer living in New York City. Her work appears in the South Shore Review and is forthcoming in *MoonPark Review*. She has an MFA in Writing from Vermont College of Fine Arts.

H. Rae Monk is a writer based in Austin, Texas. She was the first graduate from the Narrative Studies MA program at Arizona State University and holds a BA from ASU in English: Creative Writing with a focus on Fiction. Some of her favorite writers are Anthony Horowitz, Joy Harjo, Matt Goldman, Dina Nayeri, Philip Pullman, and J.R.R. Tolkein.

Lillian Morton is an MFA student who lives in Seattle, Washington. A few of her favorite authors include Ursula Le Guin, Lois Lowry, and Sylvia Plath. Her poetry has been included in *Polaris* and *Laurel Moon*. You can find her trying to recklessly spend money at Pike Place Market and looking at pictures of schnauzers on her phone.

Kait Quinn (she/her) is a Minneapolis-based poet with a B.A. in English Writing from St. Edward's University. She is the author of four poetry collections, and her work has appeared in *Reed Magazine, Watershed Review, Olney Magazine, Chestnut Review,* and elsewhere. She received first place in the League of MN Poets' 2022 John Calvin Rezmerski Memorial Grand Prize and honorable mention in the 2023 Stephen A. DiBiase Poetry Prize. She enjoys repetition, coffee shops, vegan breakfast foods, and spending time with her partner, their regal cat, and their very polite Aussie Mix.

Alli Rense is a writer, artist, and synesthete living with her family in Michigan near Lake Michigan. She has a BA in English from Grand Valley State University and works in cybersecurity. Alli writes words at night and code during the day. She adores cats, and her extra fluffy one is named Sashimi. Website: www.all.ink, Substack: whisperingvoid.substack.com, Instagram/Twitter: @allirense

William Swift is an emerging short fiction author and Caption Editor for the *Video Caption Corporation*. He is a recent graduate of the University of Sheffield, but now resides in the United States. He is passionate about paleontology, Manchester United, and exploring the little interests he uncovers every day.

Alexander Lazarus Wolff's writing has appeared in *The Best American Poetry* website, Poets.org, *The Citron Review*, *NDQ*, *The Society of Classical Poets, South Florida Poetry Journal, Main Street Rag, Serotonin*, and elsewhere. He graduated with honors from the College of William & Mary, where he won The Academy of American Poets Prize. He is a poetry editor for *The Plentitudes*. An MFA candidate, he teaches and studies at the University of Houston, where he is the recipient of three fellowships. You can find him on Facebook: facebook.com/wolffalex108/, Instagram/Twitter: @wolffalex108 and at alexanderlazaruswolff.com.

Alex Wollinka lives in Colorado Springs, Colorado, where she is studying English at Colorado College. She has interned with Dzanc Books and is currently Editor-in-Chief of *Cipher Magazine*, a student-led publication. She enjoys writing short stories and novels, and she also works as a consultant at her college's Writing Center. In her free time, Alex can be found painting, running, watching horror movies, and of course, reading. Some of her favorite authors include Kali Fajardo-Anstine, Clarice Lispector, Franz Kafka, and Neil Gaiman.

Contents:

Cover Art

Tropical Forest by Sarah Jane Walker

Black Fox Prize "Fairy Tale Remix" Winner:

Spring Fox Tales Contest "Montage of Misfortunes" Winner:

Fiction

Nonfiction

Poetry

Scarecrow Son
By Winslow Schmelling

First Place Winner of the Winter 2024 *Black Fox* Prize: "Fairy Tale Remix"

I knew we'd have a boy. A little man.

The boy he gave me was small, too small, and folded up inside of soft green cornhusk. An easy birth. I was so afraid when I didn't hear him cry, but Tate assured me.

"I can feel his heartbeat," he said, "he'll unfold when he's ready." We named him Tristan, though I struggled with the certainty of that name, feeling like I hadn't met him yet.

It was all new to us, yet sometimes it felt like Tate knew more than I did, with his own years spent caring for the corn in the field. He seemed to know when our sweet boy needed to be held, when he needed a bath. He'd run his hand through the stringy tassel at what must have been our boy's head and tell me to look how it was getting darker. I couldn't tell it was getting darker. I couldn't even tell yet that our boy was a boy. Tate would pass him to me, his palm a lingering support on the cornhusk's soft swell of a butt. I'd cradle the husk.

"Is it his hair?" I asked Tate.

"It's his silk," he said, and I envied the readiness of his answer.

When Tate would leave the room, I'd press my ear up to the boy's rough green layer, hold my breath, and listen to him. Tate told me how he'd heard his heartbeat, and I could never tell if I heard the heartbeat of my son, or my own heartbeat echoing from the tiny length of corn back into my ears. I ran my fingers over the soft yellow tassel hanging from his husk and waited patiently like a child who had discovered a cocoon. We kept him in a bassinette at night, where he slept, silent.

***

My boy, our boy, emerged from his chrysalis while we were sleeping weeks later, and I was the first to wake to his cries. This. This miniature howl was an instinct I knew, I thought. I rushed to him, alertness scraping sleep from my eyes.

His little face: flesh. I felt myself reaching for his cheeks before I truly saw him. Another kind of irresistible love, I thought. Pinch.

The husks flattened beneath him as he rolled, his little feet kicking loose from where they'd been sinched. He was pudgy, pink. I poked him, wanted to hear him react. He cried and I felt my own tears prick at the corner of my eyes.

It was then that nature took over. I knew where each palm needed to be beneath a tiny skull, beneath a tiny bottom. I cupped him, enfolded him. I ceased knowing where he stopped and where I began. He cried for so long, in this tiny, human whine, and Tate didn't wake until morning, to the both of us, a real boy and me, asleep in the armchair nearest the bricked-up fireplace.

***

Our boy was smart. Even before he could read, he'd prop encyclopedias against his knees, turn the pages, brow furrowed. He'd scour each page, eyes running in a row across the words he didn't yet know, lingering on pictures, studying up for something. He began writing before he really knew how. We'd practice the alphabet together, slow deliberation over the shape of each one. Then in the evening, he wrote me a letter, rows and rows of scribbles, except for the sign off, his name, all caps: TRISTAN. Though so often, we just called him "our boy."

Before we put him in school, the boy and I spent two hours in the store choosing the perfect backpack. He'd try one on, "Yes," I'd say, "the red suits you." He'd shift, turn, press his lips together in thought, then try on another. "Yes," I'd say, "the puppies bring out your eyes."

At school, the teachers pulled me aside to tell me how he'd made no friends so far, either in class or at recess. "We just wanted to make sure you knew. We know how the quiet ones can be." I told them I knew. I knew when I'd washed his palms in the bath, these huge blisters protruding from his skin. He told me how it was from the monkey bars, hot in late summer.

The teachers told me how he'd go back and forth, back and forth, using the whole thirty minutes of recess to heave himself across the length of the bars and back again in solitude. None of the kids would go to the monkey bars, knew it was Tristan's domain.

The blisters became regular, so some nights of the week I'd pop the bulbs of stretched flesh with a needle. They filled up every few days like bloated little mounds and I squeezed the clear liquid into a paper towel.

"Why do I have skin like yours?" he asked me, watching interestedly as the needle penetrated the thin layer of blister.

"There are some things you take after me, some things you take after your father. Some things that are also yours completely," I answered, kissing the loose skin of his now emptied blister.

"They tell me I'm not normal," he said. "That even if I look normal, they know I'm not." I sighed, swallowed his shoulders beneath my arms and held him. When I pulled away, I took his chin so he'd look at me.

"There is no future I'd wish to save you from more than being normal."

Brew
By Zelime Lewis

Winner of the Spring Fox Tales "Montage of Misfortunes" Contest

Dawn takes nine minutes to brew a pot of tea. Her time is measured in smaller increments: first, she boils the water, steeps the tea, and then adds her desired amount of sweetener and milk. Occasionally, it takes longer when she leaves the teabag in for herbal brews. But Dawn likes the constancy of the number nine—it eases her into the sharp, stinging daytime.

There are days when she sips on bitter Sencha from her China cup. Sometimes, she stirs a bright-red hibiscus brew with honey and adds ice and lemon: those days, she makes a large batch and leaves the red drink to cool in her fridge. Sometimes, she takes her grandmother's ornate crystal jar filled with demerara and stirs spoonfuls of sugar into a concoction of English Breakfast.

When she's in the kitchen and the light is blinking and everything smells like cardamom, Dawn breathes. Deeply through her nose at first, then large exhales out her mouth, tasting the lingering bitterness of tea leaves on her tongue.

Dawn thinks happiness tastes like chai sweetened with brown sugar.

Dawn cannot remember how to speak when Jonathon comes home from work. She busies herself in the kitchen, chops carrots with reckless force. When she cuts the tip of her finger, she hardly notices, only wincing when the drops of blood drip onto her freshly cut vegetables. Then, she puts her finger to her lips and sucks, she hasn't time to find a bandage.

Jonathon arrives and her finger is still in her mouth. The carrots are still only partially chopped. And Dawn stares at the blood on the cutting board. He turns on the lights that Dawn had forgotten to turn on. It's past sunset. She's been in the dark. Dawn illuminates.

"What's going on?" He asks.

When she finally finds the words, she tells him. He doesn't speak much. They eat in silence. Dawn chews caramelized carrots until they're a thick paste moving slowly down her throat. Dawn picks at the bandage wrapped around her finger. She doesn't remember putting it on.

Jonathon bangs his fist into their kitchen island until his hand is bleeding, too. Dawn gently wraps a cloth around his shaking fist when he finally settles down and has no more words left to shout.

"You're going to be such a good mother," he finally whispers into her shoulders.

Two

Dawn makes blueberry pancakes every morning for a week. Jonathon doesn't eat with her, but he swallows when she swallows. He sucks syrup off of his fingers when she sucks syrup off of her fingers. He moves and Dawn thinks of mimes wearing those strange white gloves.

When Jonathon tells her he has to cleanse her, hurt her, her lips are stained blue, and he kisses her until she's red again. Until she forgets what kind of hurt it is.

"I didn't think I needed cleansing," she says.

"This is for my family, Dawn," he replies. "This is for the safety of our child."

Once, Jonathon assured Dawn that he no longer cared for his family's approval, that it wouldn't matter. Jonathon has a picture of his family framed on his bedside table. Dawn's never met his father. They look the same. Dawn's baby will look like Dawn. She will do this ritual for Jonathon, and in return, her child will be hers, and everyone will know it.

Dawn doesn't understand it, the need to cleanse unwed mothers to protect unborn children. Movements passed down through generations of his family. She waits to hear him explain it further, and when he doesn't, Dawn just nods and swallows.

He leads her to their bedroom, his hand on the small of her back. He pulls off her shirt methodically, and Dawn lets him. Jonathon has an old knife in a wooden box hidden in his sock drawer. He takes the knife from his little wooden box, and for a singular second, Dawn thinks about asking him to wait. But she says nothing.

Jonathon's hand is steady when he holds the knife and pierces her skin just below the collarbone. It carves deep enough to draw a small amount of blood but not deep enough to make her scream. Instead, she stands still.

"I'll make you pure," Jonathon says in a voice that sounds far away. The blade moves down, under her breast, and down towards her hip bone, curving around the slight swell of her abdomen. She counts the minutes it takes him to finish.

They collect drops of blood into a jar, and Jonathon greedily dips his finger to taste her. He smiles afterward, his teeth stained red.

He puts the jar in the fridge. To keep.

When he comes back into their room, he pulls her into their shower and cleans the remnants of herself away. Dawn watches pink water turn clear, and then she steps out, staring at her fogged-up body in the mirror. Water drips down glass. Jonathon stays in the shower afterward, letting the water hit the top of his head. Dawn leaves him and unsteadily makes her way to the bed, hand resting on her stomach. She thinks maybe she should pray.

Summer has begun. She stares out the window and listens to the screeches of the birds on the trees outside. A robin calls for its mate and Dawn thinks she hears an answer somewhere in the distance calling back.

Three

When the shape of her stomach becomes something more than soft, Dawn drives thirty minutes to a gas station halfway between her mother's house and the house she shares with Jonathon. The house she owns, but Jonathon's lived in and turned into his own when he moved in with her six months ago.

Dawn's mother waits for her in the aisle by the popcorn machine and the hot dog roller. Her hair is pinned up into a tight bun. Dawn sees the bobby pins poking out and winces with memories of ballet recitals and hands around her hair. Bile rises up.

Her mother always smells of vanilla and almonds—the perfume is called *L'amour du Cyanure*. It stinks up the whole store, covering up the smell of urine and gas and stale cigarettes.

"You can see the mold on that one," Carla says, her spindly finger pointing to the hotdog on the front left side of the rotating oven. When Dawn walks up to her, they don't hug, but her hand grabs Dawn's shoulders and digs in. Both women look back at the rotating bratwursts.

Dawn watches her own body the way she watches an avatar move in a video game. Her movements are a combination of arrows and As and Bs and Xs and Ys. Her arms open out as if to hug, of their own accord.

She tells her mother she is pregnant in a voice that is not her own.

Her voice sounds like she's twelve again and her homework is unfinished.

"I knew one day we'd be here," Carla says. Eyes not reaching Dawn's. The hotdogs continue to rotate. "Is that why you insisted on meeting here? Did you think if you came home, I'd force you to stay?"

Carla's drawn-on eyebrows raise.

"You don't like Jonathon." Dawn feels her voice waver and hopes Carla hasn't noticed.

"I don't like the way he treats you."

Dawn runs her tongue across her lips and tries to taste what lingers from kissing Jonathon goodbye when he left that morning. "He treats me fine."

"He's left you before. How do you know he won't leave you again?"

Because she's let him carve into her, create life inside her, taste the blood that made her. "I just know."

"What about his family then?"

When her mother calls his family a cult, Dawn's skin starts to itch.

"I don't know," Dawn trails off. She picks up a bag of Funyuns and squeezes, feeling the crumble of dehydrated onions.

"Well, you need to think about these things when you become a parent, Dawn."

"Mom, enough." The Funyuns bag pops and drops to the linoleum floor. Both women jolt a little bit and look at the man at the front of the station. He hasn't looked up during their confrontation.

"Dawn, you're twenty-seven, pregnant, and living with a man who has been raised to believe that your unborn child is a sin! Come home with me and we will figure everything out."

Dawn eyes her mother's thin lips, frowning. "I'm not leaving Jonathon. He's happy about this. We're happy. He's not like his family. He knows better."

The bell above the gas station door jingles and two young kids race in, tumbling over each other and giggling. One sprints to the back corner where the dingy bathroom sits, stained and uncleaned. The older child paces up and down the candy aisle. Dawn sees her slip a Twix bar into her pocket but thinks to herself that a child deserves something sweet every once in a while.

Carla takes tongs and opens the hot dog machine, grabbing the moldy one up front and putting it on a paper napkin in her hand. She doesn't say anything as she walks past Dawn, past the thieving child, to the cashier at the front of the store.

"I could report you for this! Do you see what kind of food you are selling?" She waves the wiener around in the air like some kind of witch casting a spell on the poor gas station clerk, who looks at her with half-closed eyes.

If the clerk cares, he hides it well. His blue polo shirt has an oil stain shaped like a palm tree, and Dawn walks forward, staring at it as her mother chews him out. The lights in the station flicker and Dawn looks outside. It's gotten darker. She has to drive back before Jonathon gets home from work.

"—Well! I've never met a ruder man in all my life. I hope your moldy sausages poison someone and you're sued to hell and back. Dawn, come on, let's go." Carla storms out the door, the bell dinging gently.

"I spilled some Funyuns in the back, sorry," Dawn whispers to the palm tree and follows her mother outside. "I'm not coming with you," she says when she catches up to Carla.

"Of course. Right. I guess it was just wishful thinking."

They leave the decrepit station, walking away from the fluorescent lights into the gentle purple of dusk. It isn't until Carla walks Dawn to her car that she finally pulls her into a hug.

"I'm happy of course that I'm going to be a grandmother. I just wish you'd let me help you."

"It's fine, Mom."

"I really messed up as a mother, didn't I?" Carla whispers in Dawn's ears, and Dawn thinks of pirouetting.

"It's fine."

"I am trying." The hug has lasted longer than Dawn expected. Her stomach lurches.

"I know. Really, it's fine," Dawn adds for emphasis.

"I missed you."

Dawn closes her eyes and sucks in the smell of vanilla and almonds that linger behind her mother's ear. "I missed you too, Mom," she says before finally letting go.

Dawn leaves, heading back onto the highway into the city. The imprint of her mother's hug surprisingly soft against her skin. She gets home minutes before Jonathon, kissing him on the cheek when he walks through the door.

"You smell different," he tells her, inhaling sharply, looking around their kitchen for an explanation.

"Went shopping today. I tried on a couple different perfumes. Do you like?" Carla doesn't like Jonathon. Jonathon doesn't like Carla, and he would not like Dawn bringing her mother into their private lives. Not yet.

Jonathon takes another whiff, leaning into the crook of Dawn's neck. She feels his hot breath underneath her ear as he places a kiss just below her lobe and then bends to his knees, kissing the slope of her still-soft stomach. "I love it," he says as he pulls away. "I'm exhausted. Terrible day." He goes upstairs to sleep, and Dawn is left alone.

She sits in the dark on their white two-seater sofa and pulls a Twix from her coat pocket. She rips into the wrapper and tastes the chocolate and caramel. Her racing heart calms, the beat slowing to a steady rhythm. She takes another bite, the sweet on her tongue lingers.

Four

During the four minutes it takes for water to boil, Dawn closes her eyes and imagines she is a bird. She would fly away into the clouds in the distance. Making a nest of twigs and unwanted things, she would build a home from nothing. Her feathers, she imagines, glisten and change color in the wind. But then the kettle whistles.

Jonathon used to say it was silly to love tea so. He'd kiss her nose and tell her to "tone it down on the sugar."

When Dawn is alone with her tea and her thoughts, she thinks that she may not know what love means. But Jonathon always finds her before thoughts turn into something real. "My mom called today," he says while kissing her shoulder. His fingers graze where her scar turns into soft, untainted flesh.

Dawn would like to be a sparrow.

"Oh yeah?"

"Yeah. She says we should come stay with them for a few months…later, you know." He never mentions the child growing inside her, not directly.

"I thought my mom was going to come stay here." Dawn collapses into her favorite plush chair.

"In this house? No—" Jonathon's arms wave around when he speaks, like a maestro or a caricature of an Italian. He hates the lack of countertops in the kitchen, the crooked door to the bathroom, the closet that always smells like earth. He hates that the house was Dawn's before it was his. "It'll just be for a couple months. My family can help out."

"And my family can't?"

Jonathon looks at Dawn, unimpressed. "It's different with my family. You haven't met any of them yet. It would mean a lot to me if you could get over yourself and meet them."

"Exactly, I don't know them." Her voice cracks in the middle. "They're going to hate me. A *bastard* in the family.*" He used the word once, the week after she told him, when he called his parents with the news. He sobbed in Dawn's shoulder for an hour afterwards and Dawn never asked what his parents said, but his salty tears were enough of an answer.

"We'll get married, and it will be fine." Jonathon has always been a man of simple words. But proposals don't sound nice when you want to fight. "Once you're no longer pregnant, it would be too obvious if we got married now since you're already too far gone."

"Did they ask what we wanted?"

"They know what I want."

But Dawn isn't sure. Jonathon looks at his hands, ringless, and cracks his knuckles. It's an awful habit like smoking cigarettes and biting nails.

"What do you want, Jonathon?"

Eyes closed. Fingertips press into her chest, digging out arteries and blood vessels and crushing them into ash. Dawn imagines Jonathon grinning as he pulls her in and unravels her, like a ball of yarn poorly wound. Dawn wonders what he would make of her. If he would knit her back together. Make her into something no longer carrying life. If he would pull out the child still growing in her womb and unwind her too.

Jonathon has big hands, and when he rests them at Dawn's waist, it takes everything inside her not to pull away.

Five

By the time the scar begins to fade on her body, Dawn cannot recognize her reflection. It's like she's in a funhouse full of mirrors where everything is slightly wrong. Her joy shifts to something like anxiety. Feelings of maternity have yet to appear. She moves her body, pretending to make shapes she can no longer make: the bends, the curves, squatting to the ground and then moving up with ease. She practices so she can remember.

Dawn knows she's changing, like all people change, like all mothers change.

Jonathon has changed, too. He's become more excited and devoted to Dawn than ever before. Her body has never received so much attention from him. But it's attention in the way he licks his lips when she pulls off her shirt at night, her body like artwork, an outline backlit by the light of the bathroom.

Jonathon misses it—the small scar across her torso that is already becoming white from the endless amounts of ointments and creams Dawn rubs into her skin each night.

Dawn buys books upon books about babies, pregnancy, and medicine. She reads to remind herself that this is real—that she is real. While Jonathon's at work, she pours through books religiously, searching for signs.

"It's not moving," she tells him one evening as he walks through their front door. The baby is still a taboo, genderless thing making Dawn nauseous and round and angry and exhausted.

"What?" Jonathon hangs his coat in the closet behind Dawn's favorite worn chair and leans on the armrest.

"The baby. The books say I should be feeling something by now. A flutter or something."

"Don't worry. Probably just trying to scare you on purpose." Jonathon tries to smile, showing that one extra sharp canine, it glints in the dim lamplight.

Jonathon's teeth are so white, so straight and perfect, save the one extra sharp tooth that turns Jonathon into some type of predator.

"I know but what if—"

Jonathon stands up slowly, walks over, and rests his forehead against Dawn. His hand rests at her hip, his thumb grazing the bottom of her scar underneath, and Dawn shivers. "We could do *it* again?"

Dawn has seen the hungry look in his eyes each night when she steps out of the shower, she knows the reverence in his face when he traces the s-curve of the now-faded cut.

It's a superstition. Not based on science or fact, or even religion for that matter. It's an action done out of fear, and it probably won't work, Dawn knows it won't work. But all she has is fear right now and she nods her head without realizing.

He heads upstairs to read, leaving Dawn alone with half a cup of Earl Grey (unsweetened with just the slightest squeeze of lemon).

Later, when she's ready, she goes upstairs and meets Jonathon in their small room. "I'll do it. I'll do anything." He kisses her soundly and smiles, rushing to get the ornate blade, and Dawn begins to shake.

The body remembers.

This time, Jonathon cuts deeper, tracing over the faded scar. This time, Dawn allows the rage and fear inside her to bubble over and she lets out a scream. Jonathon murmurs in approval.

During the four minutes it takes for Jonathon to carve into her, Dawn imagines she is a bird.

When he goes to collect her blood, he has to find another jar. Dawn secretly threw away the other one last month when she could no longer look at the tiny drops of crimson sitting in the fridge next to her Greek yogurt. Jonathon runs to the kitchen as Dawn lies in the bed unmoving.

"You didn't do the goddam dishes, Dawn! I can't find anything to use." Dawn hears the grumbles and clanging of pots and pans as she feels her blood slowly dripping from her torso onto the mattress beneath.

And then it is silent for a moment before Jonathon returns holding a now-empty crystal jar. *Her grandmother's sugar jar.*

"I had to dump out the sugar. But it's the perfect size."

"You could have asked." Dawn thinks about the last time she put sugar in her tea: two days ago, three spoonfuls, a large mug of ginger turmeric.

"But I didn't." Jonathon sits her up to collect the blood. "It will work. I promise."

Jonathon seems certain. He'd told Dawn once about his aunt who got pregnant out of wedlock when Jonathon was only seven.

The whole family stood around her carving sin out of her body. He told Dawn how his parents prayed every night that the cutting would work, for the baby, his cousin, to be good. Jonathon hid behind his father and watched his aunt scream. When he saw his aunt cradling his little baby cousin months later, bathed in blood, he heard her thank the family around her for protecting her son.

 The next morning, Dawn feels fluttering in her stomach and curls her body inwards, suddenly thankful for the generations of women in Jonathon's family who battled before her.

Six

It takes longer for Dawn's scar to heal the second time around. The scab breaks along her hip when she tosses and turns at night. She often wakes from dreams of birds singing with the shirt sticking to her body, her dried up blood gluing the garment to her skin. When the scab is mostly receded, Jonathon buys her a bag of loose-leaf chamomile tea as a gift.

***

Dawn stares at her grandmother's vintage sugar jar in the fridge. It looks back at her, a challenge, the last drops of her sinned blood. She knows she's supposed to keep it. She doesn't really want to know why. She hasn't had sugar in her tea for a month, not since the night Jonathon cut her. When she's wanted sweet tea, she's used honey and maple syrup as a replacement. Every morning when she looks in the fridge and sees the deep red liquid in that crystal jar, she has to bite her tongue to stave off the craving for iron. Her mother told Dawn once that when she was pregnant, she craved strawberry ice cream with mayonnaise. If only Dawn wanted something so simple.

Her mother's voice speaks to her in the back of her head. "Self-control, Dawn."

All those years perfecting half-eaten meals have prepared her for this. But Dawn is hungry. Or thirsty, she can't tell.

The whistle of the kettle sings, and Dawn starts to steep some chamomile. She's left the fridge open and during the minutes it takes for her tea to steep, Dawn grabs a spoon and reaches for the crystal jar.

A cardinal hops onto a branch outside her window and stares at her. She stares back, holding her blood in her hand, and the bird nods. Dawn thinks it means something.

One spoonful couldn't hurt.

When Jonathon comes downstairs to make himself a pot of coffee, Dawn kisses him soundly, sated.

If he can taste something else on her lips, he never says.

Seven

Men used to tell Dawn that she was beautiful. Hands on leotard, skimming her fifteen-year-old skin. They'd call her words that Dawn used to not understand. Her choreographer, a man twelve years her senior, used to call her Honey after rehearsal when all the other dancers were gone, and she'd have those after-hours sessions, preparing for her solo.

His fingers were like syrup, and he knew her body more than she did.

Dawn's mother pulled her out of training when she was sixteen after seeing a constellation of small red bruises on her neck. They never spoke about it. Her mom's disappointment was measured in the weeks that sugar was banned from the house.

Now, Dawn has a man to tell her sweet things whenever she asks. Jonathon buys her chocolates every Monday evening on his drive home from work whenever Dawn says the word *craving*.

"Do you think I'm beautiful?" she asks, chocolate around her lips, licking the tips of her fingers for leftovers. A tall glass of her iced hibiscus tea looks particularly red in her hand. Dawn takes a big gulp. She tastes iron underneath the floral sweet.

Jonathon has never been poetic like her old dance trainer or those dads from back when Dawn was dainty and small. "When you're not covered in food. Of course."

Dawn sticks her tongue out at him and licks around her mouth to clean herself up. "How about now?"

"I always think you're beautiful."

Jonathon was the first person who told Dawn she was beautiful as an adult. He told her simply, without metaphor or a flurry of hushed whispers in the wings of a stage. He just said those words one morning while on their third or fourth date after he'd taken her on a strenuous hike. Dawn hadn't realized how much she'd craved a simple kind of love.

She'd been breathing heavily, her cheeks almost too red. He said it quietly at the top of a mountain before he bent down to kiss her. His voice was almost a whisper and Dawn asked him to say it again. And again. And again. And again.

Eight

"Are you afraid?" Jonathon asks in the quiet, his finger tracing the raised outline of Dawn's scar.

She can't remember when it started, when the crumbling walls of Jonathon's past self were so in ruin that she had to climb over broken things searching for parts of him. The illusion of his family had already been cracked when they met. But she thinks, in the days after he agreed to move into her home, something shattered. She's been trying to put him back together for the past year, trying to erase the shame with the smell of cinnamon sugar cookies and enthusiastic desire.

But this wasn't meant to happen. Dawn feels the child inside her kick.

Dawn's been watching her work unravel for months now, and Jonathon can't even tell that he's in pieces.

"Of course I'm afraid."

"Do you think it was worth it?" He presses his thumb to the raised point underneath her right breast. It still stings a little bit with the pressure.

"It's not my tradition, Jonathon." Dawn could placate his worries and fears. She could nod her head and say that she believes in family traditions.

Dawn's mother calls her once a week. Carla says she wants to check in with the baby, but she never asks about the baby. Instead, each week, Dawn's mother tries to make sense of Jonathon.

"I'm sorry we're not going to your home." Dawn says when Jonathon doesn't reply. His breath is loud as they lie in bed, but it's fast so Dawn knows he's still awake.

"I care about you more than them." Jonathon's been trying to prove this since he met her. He'd unwritten years of instruction, which Dawn called indoctrination, the first night he spent inside her home.

But this is a line from a script Dawn hasn't memorized yet.

"Are you excited?" she asks, to break the dialogue.

Jonathon laughs and puts the palm of his hand on Dawn's heart. His hands are large and steady and exciting. They have spent so much time over the past months tracing her ugly scar, avoiding everything else.

It's strange how a simple touch can feel like nirvana.

"I think so."

She wants to believe it.

Dawn's tea on her bedside table has cooled enough for her to drink. She dreams of crystal jars and blood and ravens and adds spoonfuls upon spoonfuls until it all tastes the same—until all she tastes is herself.

Nine

During the four minutes it takes for Dawn's water to boil, she imagines she is a bird. Dawn wants to build a nest.

The crystal jar sits, newly empty. Dawn sips on Ceylon tea that is dyed red until the mug is empty. The birds outside her window sit on nests and regurgitate worms into the stretching beaks of their young.

Dawn's water breaks before the kettle whistles.

The baby is born three weeks early.

Dawn almost dies from blood loss.

Her mother screams when she sees the faded scar set against Dawn's translucent skin. The doctors cut into Dawn, and it feels like a memory.

After

When the infant finally comes home, Carla insists it's time for her to go.

Dawn wants to tell her mother no. Her voice is dry and cracked. Every ounce of her is shedding—hair, skin, blood, sweat, tears. There isn't a big enough crystal jar to hold everything she's lost.

Jonathon and her mother never speak. They pass each other in silence.

Dawn thinks Jonathon's hands are not gentle enough to hold her daughter, but he holds her anyway.

Their front yard is thick with snowfall. The crystal jar is full of sugar. Jonathon asks for Dawn's ring size.

They name their daughter Robin.

Dawn's mother insists on doing the shopping before she leaves.

"I got you something." Jonathon is somewhere off, and Robin is asleep in their bedroom.

"Thanks, Mom." Dawn notices her mother's hair is falling loose.

She will always have scars.

"I wish I had taken care of you better." Dawn's mother's voice trembles, another inconsistency with her character.

"What are you talking about? Mom, you were a tremendous help, I don't know what we would have done without you being here this past month."

"That's not what I meant."

Dawn stands up and walks tentatively towards her mother. "Oh?"

"I failed you when you were younger. Not again."

Carla's thin hands are cold when they move to hold Dawn's face. Dawn says nothing.

"I'm so sorry." Carla kisses the top of Dawn's head. "I left your gift in the tea cupboard. Use it as you please." She makes eye-contact with her daughter for a second too long, long enough for Dawn to think it odd.

Her mom is gone before Dawn can ask what she means. She figures she's been given tea. Jonathon texts to say he'll be home in about ten minutes. Dawn starts the kettle. It takes nine minutes to make a pot of tea. She opens the cabinet.

There is a little crystal flask full of clear liquid. Dawn sniffs and smells bitter almonds and nothingness.

A New Wife's Response to the First Act
By Anne Marie Fowler

Gossamer shadows drift along the bank
where the children gather fireflies

and place them in the bamboo lanterns.
The village hums about in the night,

the fields in the distance alive
with the gentle mooing of the herd.

Next to the infusion of lotus and water lily,
the fish boats dawdle like errant children

stuck in frog mud. Left and right,
the simple life pecks like the neighbor's

chickens, unfettered by the weasel
in the rockpile. Tonight, the moon will isolate

itself from the world, render darkness
the robe of the night. Tonight, I will drink

wine from the wooden cup and confuse
my betrothed for my beloved. Even then

the fish in the stream will quiet if only
to hear the humming of my ruin.

Selected Poems by Alexa Vallejo

Ruminations

At twenty you spent your nights
at the kitchen table writing stories
about deer and car wrecks and
the collapse of the bourgeois American
family. Unmedicated, with more ambition
than talent, you struggled with plot,
filling each page with discrete moments,
scenes without scaffolding: a photo
snapped, a bad dream, ruminations
on your death. You had little to say,
but you had to say something, find
a space all your own. You pinned
your first rejection letter to your bedroom
wall, proof that someone read your work.
Older now, with words in the world,
you understand how one moment flows
into the next, how time never slows,
how chance can birth new love. Bored
of death, you chose the supple quiet
over the burning house. You learned
to let go: footsteps, a camera flash,
hoofbeats in the snow. You watched
the deer scatter, antlers wreathed with
words, fragments of a story never told.

To the Dog Who Bit Me Outside the Adams Morgan CVS

I never had any happy hour epiphanies,
glass after glass for nothing, only
a naive faith in the social contract
as I stood to go piss, leaving my
computer on the table, my belongings
always untouched when I returned.
In time I cut back, made unbreakable
rules: none today, only so much
tomorrow. Soon it was easier
to abstain than fight the urge for
more. Sobriety meant living in
the shame of a botched guitar solo
opening night. I got better, more
confident, but I missed the stupid shit:
biking into a tree, 2am Facebook stalking,
the sting of your teeth on my arm after
I placed an unwelcome hand on your
precious little head. Were you threatened
by my wine-soaked stumble, the quickness
with which I diverted course, leaned
my bicycle against the wall, and knelt beside
you? But I was always a sad drunk, slow
and lumbering, and you were a dog leashed
to a bike rack, so afraid of being left alone,
and I thought you'd see that we were the same.

Selected Poems by Tyler Wilson

Scale

death really puts the numb
          in numbers. count outbodies me.
scale is dire. baffles
          like the darkling metrics of space.

New York to whoa your windowed canyons.
drupelets in a blackberry bush.

a constellation of lungs
          scarred & tallied
& scratched into the starry ledger
          like the ceiling of his childhood.

he was curious about crying.
tried tears.

she who spoke them fluently
          as a child   imagined heaven
& pictured Costco. bright lights.
          they sold everything.

to bead a string of tenses.
to every third period an ellipsis.
to not have to mourn every end.

Ending at Evergreens

we straddle the freeway & the cemetery,
        the going   & the gone,
stroll between grass broken
      glass & fried chicken landmines

we look out over the tombstone skyline
      which kneels before the steel beyond: Manhattan
      grinning bravely
         like a kid with a missing tooth

we could never lose this, we thought

tragedy a kind of horizon
far from which we float

      like imps in the ordinary
      miracle of relative peace,   collecting
        audaciously
          delicate things:

a language of our own like hummingbird bones
plans like origami
the humble scaffolding
    of a kiss

Memories in the Rearview
By Angela Kirby

"You and I were supposed to be/ Until the end of the time/ Who knew the end of time/ Would come from two pink lines/ Now all we are is memories/ Memories in the Rearview."

I stabbed the radio's power button silencing my own voice. I had never wanted to hear one of my own songs less. I didn't need the extra reminder of where I was headed. The drive back to my one stoplight town was already churning up memories I was reluctant to deal with. Years ago, I packed up my car, said goodbye to the farm I called home, and drove west for a chance at something more. I didn't know what was ahead for me, but I knew all I was leaving behind were days working at the feed store and nights spent at Dusti's listening to the jukebox while dancing with fading football stars.

Now, I drummed my fingers against the steering wheel of my rented SUV hoping the improvised beat would drive away memories threating to surface in the quiet aftermath of my song. The drive from town to my dad's went by faster than I remembered. At the end of the gravel driveway, the farmhouse stood illuminated with windows and porch lights giving a welcoming warmth to the darkness.

I parked and got out of the car. No voices. No traffic. Just the whisper of wind, the orchestra of crickets, and the creak of the old tire swing hanging from the branches of the towering oak in the front yard. I looked towards the house where my family was, but I headed in the direction of that tree. I had spent countless hours underneath its branches dreaming of what my life could be. My fingers trailed against the rough bark as I looked around the place I had called home.

"Can I help you?" someone called from the front door.

My heart skipped like a record needle finding its groove as I took in the tall figure backlit by the porchlight. "Landon," I said, more to the tree than to him.

"Jacelyn." His voice conjured up stolen moments in hay piles, wind whipping through my hair as we rode horses, and nights spent in the bed of his truck watching the stars above.

"What're you doing here?" I asked as I moved towards the porch. The closer I got, the more of him I could make out. He had always been tall, but he had filled out over the years. I made out the corded muscles of his arms and shoulders under the thin fabric of his shirt.

"Dropping something off for your dad. What are you doing here? The wedding isn't until Saturday night."

His words put me on the defensive. "I'm surprising my dad."

"I think everyone'll be surprised. Surprised you showed up at all. Some of us figured you'd never come back."

He'd had years to sharpen his attack. I resented his implication, that I left him like my mother left my dad, but I couldn't argue with his logic. I might never have come back to him, but I'd do anything for my dad. "I wasn't going to miss my dad's wedding, and I've never not shown up for my family."

"There was more here than just your family, but I guess those memories were only useful when you were writing songs about memories in the rearview."

I bristled at the bitterness as he threw my own song lyrics back at me. I wanted to tell him he didn't own those memories. They were my memories too, and if I wanted to write songs about them I could, but my words died on my lips as the door behind Landon swung open.

"Landon, who are you—Jacelyn!"

Before I could reply, my older brother, Jeremy, was flying off the porch, and I was wrapped in his arms, then swung off the ground. "What are you doing here? Maggie and Dad are going to be so surprised."

His words broke the storm brewing between Landon and me. I let Jeremy guide me towards the house and up the porch. I tried to keep my gaze on the front door, but like a compass needle pulled north, my eyes went to Landon. His whiskey gaze was hidden in the shadows of the porch as he stepped back to avoid me.

I pulled out of my brother's grasp as boot steps fell down the porch stairs behind us. "Jeremy, I'll be in in a second," I said.

I leaned over the railing, watching Landon head for his truck. "You don't have to leave," I called into the darkness.

He stopped, turning towards me. "I can't stay."

Those words. The air vibrated with memory, and I was eighteen again. He was standing in front of me asking me to stay, making promises of what our lives would be like if I just gave him a chance. But all I had heard at the time was the whoosh of tires on the road out of town and the vibrations of an electric guitar guiding me to my destiny. So, I said I couldn't stay and left him behind.

Now he was the one leaving, and I was left watching his taillights disappear down the drive.

I walked into the house. It smelled like peach cobbler and pot roast. Voices drifted towards me from the kitchen, but I stood in the entranceway looking at the scarred wood floor and the banister that led upstairs. Memories tumbled around me. Jeremy and I thundering down those stairs on Christmas morning, my father standing at the foot of them silently watching my mother gather her bags, and Landon staring up at me on prom night, a huge smile on his face.

"Jacelyn get in here," my dad called from the kitchen.

He sounded happy, and I was happy for him. Happy Maggie came along and changed his world, but my world was reeling, and I wasn't ready to face my family yet.

"In a minute," I called back. I needed to get my bearings. I hadn't expected to see Landon so soon. Hadn't expected to want to run to my car and hightail it back to California. I walked up the stairs towards my room. The banister smooth under my hand. The stairs creaking under my weight.

At the top, immediately to the left was my bedroom. Opening the door was like walking back to seventeen again. Posters of rock bands hung on the walls. Pictures of me and my friends stuck in the frame of the mirror above my dresser, and my dad's guitar, the one he had taught me to play on, hung on the wall.

The room smelled like lemons and summer. The bed was freshly made, and there wasn't a layer of dust on anything. I walked towards the window that faced the oak tree. I couldn't begin to count the number of times I scrambled across the roof of the porch to meet Landon.

"Hey, Firefly. This is a nice surprise." My dad's voice broke into my thoughts.

I smiled at the name and turned to look at him. He was tan and his face had a few more lines since last Christmas, but his eyes sparkled and there was a huge smile on his face. "That's what I was hoping for." I watched him take in me standing in a room I hadn't set foot in for twelve years.

"How's it feel being home?" he asked.

"Strange. I wasn't expecting to find it exactly the way I left it," I said.

My dad chuckled. "Not actually the same. I cleaned it up a bit, but I wanted it to be ready. I knew you'd come home eventually."

"At least one of us did," I said, as I took in my room again.

"How about we leave the memories alone for a bit, and we get you some dinner. I'm assuming you're hungry."

I shrugged. "I could eat."

"Glad some things haven't changed." He wrapped his arm around my shoulder, and we headed downstairs.

***

I let out a huge yawn as I looked over the rolling summer-green hills dotted with horses and white fences. I had forgotten the early hours that were kept around here, and the cup of coffee I had this morning was wearing off—along with the shock of learning the wedding was happening at Landon's farm. I took in all the buildings on Landon's property. The barns had been fixed up. The farmhouse with its wrap-around porch had a fresh coat of paint. Landon had done it. He had taken his grandparents floundering horse farm and turned it around.

I looked at the stables and was bombarded with memories of helping Landon and his grandpa take care of the horses. The renovated barn behind me was filled with the voices of Maggie's friends and family as they turned it into a country wonderland of rustic wood, lace, twinkle lights, and lanterns. But it was also filled with memories. Me sitting on a pile of hay as Landon worked on his truck, us slow dancing to songs on the radio, and him kissing my neck as I wrote songs while we laid tangled up together on a flannel blanket in the loft.

"Everything good in there?"

I turned towards the crunching gravel and deep timber of his voice. My mouth went dry as Landon walked towards me. Jeans clung to his thighs, and his shirt sleeves were rolled up, showcasing his muscular forearms. Boots and a backwards baseball cap completed the look. He looked eighteen but so much better.

"We're good. I was taking a minute to admire what you've done with the place."

Landon looked around at the buildings. "Yeah, I bet it looks a bit different than you remember it."

I shook my head. "No, not so much, but you did it." I couldn't keep the pride out of my voice. "I just…I just wasn't expecting all of this." I swung my arms out, taking in everything.

Landon always wanted to revitalize his grandparents' business after his dad tanked it. But to see it now, thriving? It was impressive, and I was happy for him.

Landon ducked his head and rubbed his neck. "I know all about unexpected. Last night, I'm sorry."

"Don't worry about it. I get it."

"I'm sure you do."

Silence stretched between us. So many things needed to be said, but I didn't know how to ask him if he still hated me for making the choices I made. If he would've rather had the family he'd planned with me or if was he happy with how his life turned out? I looked around the property again. "You did good, Landon. I'm sure your grandparents would be proud."

"They got to see some of it, and they were proud of me…and you. Granma loved hearing your songs on the radio. She'd always ask me to play them, even if she didn't understand your love for rock and roll."

His words were a bittersweet sting. His grandparents always treated me like family, but I had left them behind too. "I can still hear her calling for me to stop with that rock music and sing her a country song."

"Dad!" A young boy's voice interrupted the conversation.

We both turned. The Landon from my childhood stood next to the stables, and as I snuck a glance at my Landon, I saw pride in his eyes. He really had gotten everything he wanted, even if it hadn't been with me.

"So, that's Lucas."

His eyes widen at my words. "It is."

"Don't look so surprised. Dad and Jeremy kept me up to date. I might not have come home, but that doesn't mean I didn't know what was happening."

"Dad!" Lucas called again, not giving Landon a chance to comment on the revelation that I had been keeping track of him.

"I better go see what he needs," Landon said.

I nodded and watched him walk away. Watched him walk towards something he had wanted and I wouldn't give him, then instead found with Kerri Adams. I had been shocked when six months after I left, Jeremy told me Landon and Kerri got married. I had been hurt when I heard Landon had a son with her, but I hadn't been surprised to hear they had gotten divorced.

Now, all I felt as I watched Landon walk into the stable with his hand on his son's shoulder was the tug of regret. It felt uncomfortable and heavy. So, I did what I always did when I felt the melancholy of what might've been tugging at me. I shut my eyes, took a deep breath, and focused on where I was going—and where I was going now was back into that barn full of memories to finish getting it ready for my dad's wedding.

***

The barn rocked with music and laughter as I watched my dad twirl Maggie around the dance floor. Their wedding ceremony had been simple family and a few close friends, but the reception was lively and filled with touching speeches and bawdy jokes. I took in a deep breath pulling in the sweet scent of honeysuckle and hydrangeas, but underneath those I got the faint whiff of fresh cut hay and grass. I hadn't been prepared for how nostalgic I'd feel coming home. As I stood on the edge of the dance floor watching friends and family celebrate my dad and Maggie, I realized I missed this place more than I ever let myself feel once I had left.

The music shifted to a slow song, and I paused at the familiar chords. My heart clenched as lyrics I knew as well as my own came from the speakers. Without missing a beat, my eyes found Landon across the dance floor. We moved toward each other. Drawn together by words and memories. As he stood in front of me with his hand extended, I was powerless to resist not only the song, but the smile on his face.

I placed my hand into his calloused palm, and he drew me to him. Being in his arms felt like coming home.

"Haven't listened to this song in years," I said.

"Me either. I'd shut it off or leave the room," he said.

"I'm sure this isn't the only song you've done that with," I said.

"If you mean your songs, not always. When I was mad, yeah." He gathered me tighter against his chest. "But sometimes, I liked hearing your voice."

My fingers traced the lines of his shoulders as we swayed together listening to lyrics about being young and in love.

"We had some good times," I said.

"We did."

I closed my eyes and rested a cheek on his chest as the song washed over us. Tears pricked my eyes as lyrics about getting pregnant and growing up wrapped around us. I wanted to push away from him, but Landon's arms banded tighter around me.

"I don't hate you anymore. I haven't in a long time. I get why you made the choice you did." His voice was a rough whisper against the delicate skin of my ear.

"You do?"

I felt him take a deep breath. "We were kids in an impossible situation."

"You were never a kid, but you're right. We wouldn't have made it."

He didn't answer me. We swayed together till the end of the song, and I let Landon lead me off the dance floor. We were quiet as we headed in the direction of Landon's house. The noise of the reception fell away as we walked up the steps of the porch. We stood next to each other looking out over the property. The lights from the wedding reception filled the night with an amber cast.

I turned towards him. "I'm sorry my decision hurt you. I loved you so much. I didn't want to grow to resent you like my mom did with my dad."

He looked down at me. I didn't see anger or hurt in his eyes. I saw understanding. "I know that now, but I didn't back then. I thought we would've been different, that we would've made it. And maybe we would have." Landon moved closer to me.

His arm brushed against mine, and I felt a jolt of warmth and anticipation at the touch. It reminded me of when I was seventeen and our relationship was blossoming.

"Maybe. Or maybe we would've broken under the weight of responsibility, lost dreams, and feelings of being trapped," I said.

"You were always destined for something better than this town."

I shrugged. "I don't know about that, but I do know I wanted something more than this town, and I'm sorry if you thought that meant I wanted something more than you. If we had been older. If we had already lived our lives. It might've been different, but we were kids, and I made the decision that I thought was best. There have been times I wondered what might've been, but even if I could go back, I wouldn't change my choice."

He nodded and looked away. I felt bad for the truths I had given him, but I couldn't be anything less than honest. I put my hand on his, pulling his attention back to me. "It makes me happy to see that you got what you wanted in the end."

"I did. But you're right. It was hard. Harder than I ever imagined."

"Is that what happened with you and Kerri? Was it too hard?" I asked.

Landon looked at me. I was caught in his gaze.

"It was too hard being married when the past was never quite gone. Too hard living with the idea of what should've been," he said.

I knew he meant me. Meant us. "I suppose I should say I'm sorry for that as well."

"No reason to apologize. Kerri always said she knew what she was getting into, but when she asked for the divorce, she said it was because she deserved to be someone's first choice. I couldn't fight that. It's hard to compete with the past."

I speared my hands through my hair ruining the curls I had labored over. "Whew…that was…" my voice trailed off. It had been heavy, but I felt lighter than I had in years.

"I know," Landon said.

Music, conversation, and laughter floated towards us on the summer breeze. I looked toward the barn where my family was celebrating, then back at Landon. "What'd ya say we go make some new memories?"

Landon looked at me, a spark in his eyes that I hadn't seen in twelve years. A smile tugged at his lips. He held out his hand, and I slid my palm against the rough skin of his, letting him lead the way.

***

Morning sun streamed through the windows as I sat up in bed. I smiled to myself as memories from last night fell around me. Landon and I dancing to country songs, laughing at childhood stories my dad told, singing at the top of our lungs, and strolling together through the horse stable after we closed the wedding down.

I tingled all the way to my toes as I thought about him brushing a stray lock of hair from my eyes—the moment when the past, present, and future fell away, and it was just us. I wanted to curl under the covers wrapped in the scent of Landon's spicy cologne and the warmth I found in his bed. I didn't want to face reality or the possibility of running into Lucas, but I couldn't hide forever.

I swung my legs out of bed and found that Landon had picked up my dress at some point and folded it over the back of the chair. I smiled at the sweetness of the gesture.

I padded down the stairs to the quiet first floor. Landon was in the kitchen cleaning some dishes. My heart skipped a beat as he looked over his shoulder and smiled at me. I couldn't stop myself from thinking about how this could've been my future.

"Morning. Coffee?" he asked.

"Please." I stepped up to the island. "Where's Lucas?"

Landon handed me a mug, and I took a sip. It was how I liked it with cream and sugar.

"He spent the night with friends. I'm not sure I'm ready for him to know I had an overnight guest."

"I would've liked to meet him officially," I said, and I meant it. "You don't have a lot of overnight guests then?"

Landon smiled. "You'd be the first. Feels kind of right that way."

It was my turn to smile this time. "I guess I've tarnished your perfect dad reputation."

"You're worth a little tarnish," he said, "maybe next time though."

I liked the banter. It made me feel like we were teenagers flirting under the oak tree. "Next time?" I asked.

"You never know. It could happen."

I nodded. "You're right it could. I wish I could stay longer, but—"

"The real world calls. I never expected you to stay."

His words cut deeper than I wanted them too, because I did want to stay. I wanted to get to know this version of Landon, and his life now, but I couldn't. I had a tour and a new record to promote. I didn't say that though. Instead, I took another drink before setting my cup down.

"Let me walk you to your car." He placed the mug in the sink.

The walk to my car was silent. I wanted to say how much last night meant to me. How much it meant that he wasn't angry with me anymore. But I didn't. I let the silence sit between us because I wasn't ready to admit that last night hadn't felt like saying goodbye, but rather hello.

We reached my car, and I looked at him framed in the morning light. He was golden. I stepped towards him, and he opened his arms. I sank into his hug and his warmth.

"Don't take so long to come home again," he said.

I breathed him in, making sure to imprint everything about him to my memory. "I'll try," I said. I didn't want to make a promise I wasn't sure I could keep.

"It's better than nothing."

I slowly let him go. Not taking my eyes off of him as he opened my door, and I slid inside. I looked in my rearview as I drove away, Landon watching me leave again. This moment felt the same and different. We had been here before, but things had changed. We had changed. I had changed. But we would always be more than memories in the rearview.

Brick
By Devon Neal

The ghost that haunted my nightmares
was the nail-black figure of a tornado,
the type that picked up Dorothy's house.

It lurked in the shadows of every storm,
coiled in the wisps of thunderclouds,
waiting to drop, its voice shaking

the walls of my childhood bedroom. Mom said
our brick house could stand against the wind
and our basement, pooled from vein cracks

could protect us. I read books about them,
the way they could impale trees with 2x4s
and doubted. In spring, I inspected our brick,

the tight gray tendons holding it together.
On the radar, storms spread like a disease,
redness swelling, sweeping south

where, in my lightning-brightened bed,
I pictured the house tightening, leaning
against the insistence of the wind,

holding together in the sheets of rain. Doubt came
from my mouth, shouting for her in the dark,
but the house stood. Wind shook windows,

and once, lightning came in through the wires
and turned the TV into a globe of light.
Doubt came. The house stood.

I don't know how many tornadoes
tested the brick while I slept.
Storms came once and carried my father away,

but still she came in the night and told me
it's only thunder, it's already passing,
and our house is standing, still.

Chiaroscuro
By Sarah Rachael Johnnes

Shrouded by echoes, she twirls away her storm. She drank
wind as she yelled into hollowness. The weight of despair
could be equal to the weight of hope. But I don't think so.
There are gravitational pulls and unforeseen torques. She
is on repeat like a worn needle skipping on a record hearing
the same partial lyric. Over and over. Counterbalance.
They say you can't have one without the other. But I don't
think so. Sometimes the loop is twisted steel coils with
no forgiveness. The weight of despair is a patina of
dashed hopes on dusty skin; wishing to be husked.

Christened Red
By Carolina Mata

Your new foster mother walks you through the local store. Local to her, not you. You came from three hours away.

"You take something and put in purse or put in pockets, I tell security you not mine," your foster mother says, "I go home and leave you." She shakes her finger theatrically, and you wonder if she's always this angry or just today? Not a full one day in her care and she's already frustrated with the language barrier of her broken English and your pathetic Spanish. This isn't your first foster family with this issue, and you're reminded of your failures as a properly assimilated kid.

Her teenage sister lives with her, too. Daisy. Daisy just got her student visa and speaks even less. But she smiles a lot, and that's new, you think.

She stops at a row of boxes. Green. Lavender. Pink. All pastel.

"You bleed?" She makes a sweeping motion to your crotch and then the boxes.

Your neck is hot. You shake your head. Not yet, and you wonder when. You're twelve already, the ripe age, as your last foster mother said. Your new mother walks you onward now. And you want to apologize for not being ripe yet. Daisy shakes her head.

***

This foster mother likes things clean. You realize this as you settle in. The house is decorated in white—white sofas, white pillows, white picture frames, and a glass dinner table with porcelain legs. White staircase and white crown molding. White tiles in every room on the first floor and white carpet on the second. The house smells of bleach as she wipes everything down four times each. You don't understand her process of four times each.

Daisy sweeps, washes dishes, and laundry, which is two chores more than you have, but she's always done before you. You don't know if it's because she's fast, used to the pace of cleaning cleaning cleaning, or if your task is just that more time consuming.

Your chore is to mop. But you've never mopped like this before. You're instructed to take four rounds over the floor of each room, each night.

The first round: mop with fresh, soapy water.

The second: wring the mop until it's dry and go again, getting all the suds.

The third: take the bucket out to the backyard and pour it into the sand. Fill it with fresh water, making sure to rinse it out good. Then mop with fresh, clean water.

The fourth: rinse the mop itself—get out all the suds—and wring it dry (as dry as you can). Then go over the floor again. Soak up any water and use a towel with your hands if you have to.

Once you're done, she comes downstairs from her nap to check for streaks. She circles the floor to look at every angle. If there are streaks, you have to do it again. "Because we do not live in filth," she says. She yells as she points them out to you. But you can't see them. You go over it again anyway.

***

The week you move in, a neighbor brings a casserole. "You're a saint," she tells your foster mother. "I couldn't take in," she whispers, "strange children."

She looks at you with pity, then disgust, then fear. Your foster mother smiles in a way you haven't seen yet, in a way you didn't think she could, all bright eyes and loosened shoulders. Light voice and flushed cheeks. The picture of PTA royalty.

When the neighbor leaves, your foster mother announces, "All the mothers love me here. I put up with kids like you."

And it finally hits you why she really chose this.

***

You panic at the brown. You've never seen it before. Not in your underwear. Not like this. Despite years of waiting, the situation doesn't occur to you. It's the color that throws you. As you stare, you remember the first time you felt wetness down there, back when you were six. Back when you touched inside and felt stickiness that was thicker and, when you pulled your hand out, whiter and more sour smelling than sweat. You panicked then, too. But as you ignored it, got used to it, accepting it as something your body just did, you seemed fine. Now, as the memory lingers, you wonder: is this what you've been waiting for?

You look at the dark smudges. This isn't the image you dreamt of as a kid—an image of red, dripping, a dainty pool at your feet. You gather paper around two fingers and push inside. The first time, there's brown and yellow, like dried mud and leaves. The second time, the color is almost gone but for a sickly spot of almost green. The third, nothing. Clean. You pull your jeans up and go about your day. Before bed, you check again. Still clean.

***

You wake with it all over you. Finally, the red, comically bright red, the sticky puddle on the sheets. You run and thin rivers streak down. You pat paper around, amazed at the tacky consistency of semi-dried ink. It's deep in every crevice of your flesh and folds. Over your bottom. Your lower back. Even your chubby stomach is somehow unclean. No amount of paper wipes away the brown, the red, the pink.

Daisy finds you crying at the sink. She calls your foster mother. There's embarrassment over your neck and cheeks, glistening smudges on your forehead. She screeches.

"Now you have to shower." She has no sympathy. She refuses to touch your bedding. You put them in the wash yourself. "You miss the bus," she says. "Now I have to drive you." She throws a pad at you and says to hurry. You've never put one on before. Never seen it done. Daisy offers to show you, but you decline. You're not a kid, after all. Not anymore. You read the thin pictures on the box and take too long. Now, there's more to clean up. Again. More screeching. Daisy hands you a wet towel.

***

The pads are itchy. Take up too much space. You see them through your clothes. You think everyone else can see them, too. Everyone else must know. Your lower back twitches. You want to scream. You don't know why you want to scream. The twitching increases. Your shoulders feel sore. Your skin's too tight. Your clothes are too tight. You imagine taking a flaying knife and skinning yourself like dinner salmon. (Then maybe everything wouldn't be so damn tight.) There's crawling in your skull, like roaches moving below your hair, scattering to your neck, making you jump. At night you scratch your skin raw. You squirm. You bite the pillow. You smother sobs.

***

You wake with a sense of peace. You don't know where it comes from. You don't question it. This is what you've been waiting for. Is this triumph? You can belong now. Belong where, though? That's the real question. Why hadn't you thought to question it before?

You think of all the stories told, how you're now supposed to be *apart*. You're supposed to exist among the billion hordes of "blooming women," a former foster mother once said. A "sisterhood," connected forever, a teacher once said. You are one grain of sand among the beach. Just as equal. Just the same. Indiscernible from the rest. You stand among many. You must've heard that somewhere before, too, but you can't remember where.

Is that what they mean when they say "family"? Is that how it happens? Even with those you've never met. Is this what it means to belong?

You listened to all the chatter, the PE conversations as a kid, and you didn't think to ask for follow ups then. But now, thinking of all those you overheard, learned from, that you never saw again, (thinking of yourself laying in a city you don't know, with people you know you won't see for long either, because it's never for long) you have a feeling in your gut that not all of these sayings are true.

Something's missing in the logic. So many things.

These are outdated notions for little kids and old women, you think. Not for those in the present (the grounded in the pain of reality present). You want to cry. You don't know why. You don't let yourself.

Then you stand. The pool is there again. Now almost purple. So dark. So thick. As if you could almost bleed out of life overnight.

You remember the anger of your foster mother the day before, the inconvenience that you were. So, you make the bed, following the rules of this house, pulling the comforter over wet sheets. Laundry day is two days away, on Saturday. If you volunteer for the chore, she doesn't have to know. She may even be pleased. She might even say, "good." Good.

You clean yourself in the bathroom, little blobs and chunks falling out into your hand, slippery against your skin. It takes you forever to get it all clean, but you hope it'll all be well.

She finds the mess while you're at school. Apparently, she checks your bed and drawers every day, and you never even knew.

"You're disgusting," she says. "Lying in filth like that."

***

You learn quick that you can't just put a pad on and ignore it for the day. In just an hour the blood flows in a single line from the center to over your underwear, leaking through the fabric. It feels like a waste. The whole thing doesn't even get stained, but you have to throw it away anyway. Just to avoid a leak. You take off the old one, wrap it in paper until it's covered—no more red to be seen—and throw it away, just like Daisy showed you.

One night your foster mother yells for you. "You have no shame?" she asks, and you don't know how to respond. "You just leave blood in trash and for all to see?"

But you're confused. She points at the can, and you see the thick wrap of paper. Your pad, mummy style. There are tiny spots of red peeking through. "What if your brother was here?" She mentions the brother you once had. The one who aged out and disappeared. Probably forever. Like most older siblings do.

"You want him to see that?" she asks.

You take out the trash.

***

Your social worker sits at the dinner table, coffee in hand. He compliments your foster mother on how clean the house is, how beautiful and shiny. The whole house smells of purple Fabuloso and window cleaner. It took you and Daisy hours to get it this spotless. He says her taste is chic. And she smiles that bright smile you've only seen with the neighbor. And again, you wonder if it was her life purpose to offer coffee cakes at glass tables and polished chairs.

Then your foster mother tells him all about the blood. The sheets she has to wash every day because you haven't learned how not to leak yet, she says. "That's how the diseases spread. She's going to make us sick." Daisy pours him more coffee while you stand, arms and back straight, as was expected for a scolding, and she hunches her shoulders like she wants to disappear, too.

He looks awkward. Unsure how to respond. He clears his throat and doesn't look at you while he says that you need to have good hygiene, that you need to keep your bed clean. That you can't be sloppy in life. You stand against the wall. You look at the white coffee mugs that Daisy will have to bleach to get the stains off once he leaves, too ashamed to raise your head.

"No dessert for you," she says once he's gone. She plops ice cream in her bowl, another for Daisy who's finished the dishes without you even seeing. "No dessert until you don't leave stains." You look at Daisy, tall and thin. Who doesn't even like vanilla ice cream and often tries to convince her sister for chocolate instead. She shrugs. You don't know how to interpret that.

***

You clench your thighs tight at night. Two pads, back-to-back, with paper wrapped around your underwear. You create a makeshift diaper. You force yourself awake. If you drift off, you might turn over and leak. You doze off and stain anyway. No dessert and now no dinner.

Two weeks a month, your only meal is school lunch. You ask Daisy if hers lasts this long, and she shakes her head. You're tempted to ask the nurse if this is normal, but you think it is. You remember vague comments from Sex Ed about "everyone is different." You watch the other kids. You have the urge to beg them for leftovers. But you don't.

***

You train yourself to stay awake all night and clean yourself every hour. Even if you doze off, you wake up on time. Your body knows now. Your mind is stronger. The red flashing clock is your countdown. You suffer headaches from lack of sleep, lack of food, the heat of the city, the frustration of being unclean.

You try to tell your social worker once, but he stops you. He says kids have been coming to your foster mother for years. All of them, bad. But she puts up with them. "She doesn't have to take you in," he says.

He reminds you that there are worse parents out there, like your own. He reminds you of the horror stories you've heard of before, the parents that beat, that neglect, that abuse. Your foster mother isn't the same, he says, and technically he's right. She doesn't beat or pimp or leave for days on end.

"So, try being a little more grateful," he says. "Be good." Be good. You think of Daisy, who never makes your foster mother angry. In fact, she's so good, your foster mother lets her have a glass of wine with her at the end of the day, despite being nineteen. Daisy never complains. Never leaks. Never does anything but what she's told and stays out of the way, making her tall frame so small, it's difficult to realize when she's there. She goes to community college and does well despite her language barrier. Daisy is good.

***

You promise to be good when your foster mother goes out. You and Daisy are left alone.

"No mopping," she says.

"She'll be mad if I don't," you say.

"Later. Together. Right now, ice cream." She takes out the forbidden tub. You're not allowed to watch TV. Not in this house. But you sit on the white couch and hold a remote for the first time in months. You try to translate the show with your hands for Daisy. She laughs. You laugh. It feels nice.

When you stand, your bowl falls. It breaks with a clash. There's red on the couch. But you hadn't leaked in days. You were so good. You try so hard to be good. Daisy holds you when you cry. Your body shakes. You scream into her neck. You don't know if she can understand your babble, and you don't even really know what you're trying to say. But you want to explain, to everyone, you tried so hard. She nods, like she's listening.

She scrubs the blood as well as she can. The pink suds stain her nails. You watch from the floor, surprised at how she doesn't care. Unlike her sister, who refuses to touch your sheets.

She tells your foster mother the blood was hers. She receives the shouting that should've been yours. You listen as you brush your teeth for the night. "What'd she say?" you whisper at the sink when it's over.

"Mama showed us better. Better than bleed everywhere. Like a whore." She says the last word with emphasis. You don't understand the connection.

"How is bleeding like being a whore?" you ask.

"Both are dirty," she says. "Mama said."

You want to apologize. You're not sure why or what for. But you imagine their mother and wonder if she shouted for whiteness or scrubbed with stained hands. But Daisy smiles and shakes her head before you can ask. "If mama saw us now," she says.

***

It's the day before your move to a new home. You don't know where yet. You feel the familiar wetness of a new month and go to the bathroom to start your routine of sleep deprivation. But Daisy is there. When she opens the door, she pauses to look at you. She looks down, at the pad in your hand. "New month," she says.

"New blood," you say.

She turns and reaches beneath the sink. You watch her pull out the boxes of pink, blue, and green. The pastel boxes. You ask her what she's doing, but she shakes her head. With long fingers, she takes the one from your hand. The wetness feels slicker between your legs. You wonder if she is finally being cruel. Like so many other siblings in other homes can get, eventually.

"I'll make a mess," you say. The words are tight. Your chest, heavy. You don't like to cry. And you think she's crazy for not knowing the consequences. But she hugs you, one armed, and you resist the urge to grab the boxes that are in the other because, although you want a pad for a night, you really don't get hugs very often. And this is nice.

"Your last night," Daisy says. And you nod. This is your last night in the bleached and shiny house. You don't know whether to celebrate for the end of your foster mother or dread for whatever might come worse. It always gets worse, is the foster kid phrase. But Daisy repeats, "Your last night."

"So?"

"So, make a mess," she says.

You want to argue but you remember your birthday night. Just last month. You puked while mopping. The little bit of food you had all day. It's something you do now, when the bleeding comes, get so nauseated you can't keep your stomach right. The dinnerless punishments for leaking didn't help. You were so sluggish. So exhausted. Waiting for the screams that would come. You were so afraid.

Lying in bed, you force yourself to stay put and sleep. When your body wakes, trained, you turn over. You slow your breathing. You will not be good, you think. The next morning, there's the smallest smudge on the linen. Not as big as you expected or as big as others in the past. But you make the bed without changing the sheets, as you once did. You clean yourself. Not with wet paper, that bunches and crumbles, but with a white towel. One you know you're not supposed to use. You don't rinse it either. You leave a smudge on the seat.

Anxiety clenches your stomach. You can't breathe. You ignore it.

You wash your hands. You leave the pink droplets in the sink. You want traces of it everywhere, you think. On the white porcelain, on the white furniture, on the white tiles of the floor, on the white banister of the white carpeted stairs.

You want to christen this place with your red.

What will she do? Chase you down to your new foster home just to scream? Let her scream. Let them know what kind of a mother she is. What kind of neighbor, who only smiles when she's praised and only cares when there's coffee to serve.

Suitcase in hand, you pass Daisy's room. She holds you tightly for a second, then closes the door. She doesn't meet your eyes. You know you will never see her again and you think of the pink stains of your blood on her nails.

Your foster mother kisses your forehead. Something she's never done before, and only to Daisy when she's been extra fast at sweeping or brought a good grade from college. You want to swipe it away. But you don't.

"Good luck" she says. She smiles.

"Thank you," you say. You smile. It's an empty exchange. You know. You did not see bright eyes in her smile.

In the car, your social worker talks about your new home to come. You'll be taken to the next town over, barely in the county. "Be good," he says. Always be good. But you're not listening.

You picture the red on your sheets. Your foster mother's face. The way *it* will redden at her discovery. The way it plumps and flushes when she screams. And you feel the slightest breath of satisfaction, and terror, as you drive away.

again
By Alexis Jaimes

whenever it's cold I feel you too
the distance between us and the time back then shortens
the horizons change but the atmosphere smells familiar
my joints ache
spine shrivels
an exhale spreads out against a bruised skyline

it feels like home away from home again
the numbness begins to wear off

I am tender again
I am vulnerable to those feelings I thought were extinct ages ago
trapped in slumber running down untouched cheeks

it smells like menthol cigarettes again
my head grows lighter
only I don't hesitate to inhale the secondhand
I try to keep it in
I don't want any trace of you to leave
but
I cough like I always did

my eyes are red again
surrounded in saltwater
I rub the sentiment off onto a rolled fist
I see shards of light looking like pieces of broken glass
because nothing ever remains intact
not even this

it feels like last time

my words loiter in the space between us
heavy with desperation sinking into oblivion
like we always did

then
you're gone

again

Selected Poems by Emily Hoover

Lines Composed on the Morning After You Left Me

The last time I was in this cactus forest, I knew
with certainty that it wanted to kill me: I fished
sand spurs out of my socks, was body checked
by concealed chollas, used a barber's comb
to pull cactus burrs from Gretel's fur,
& heard the *rattattat* of a rattlesnake
under a shrub. Take warning.

After the fire, I wonder: did we kill the forest?
Gretel's leash draws a snaking line in the charred
sand. Joshua trees painted like dairy cows.

& then, a barrel cactus: sun drunk
& blooming marigold; & then, a Joshua leaf
sprouting from the carcass of a yucca; & then,
you on your knees, inspecting rocks like a child
& placing them in my hands like beads
from a broken bracelet, the forest alive in your eyes.

The Match We Lit

The sky was charcoal, sugar sand so cold as it crept through webbed spaces between my toes. I didn't know we were on fire though I could smell burning flesh, hair, plastic. The sky was bright with forgiveness, a false sense of stillness, of stirring, of change. I didn't know we were on fire though I could see smoke of the dead thing dancing near Point Loma's edge: split of sea from rock, submarine base from air station. The sky was cotton candy, not fulfillment but vanity, not alive but charming—a taxidermic love. I didn't know we were on fire though I could hear the crackle of the dead thing as it smoldered, sand growing colder. The sky was yellow with sickness. I saw in the distance the match we lit, the stringy smoke. I only knew we were on fire when I could taste embers piercing my throat, choke on smoke, run my tongue across severed skin on the roof of my mouth, feel heat melting my body. And I knew we were dead. I decided to swim.

The Laboratory Worker as an Animal Model for Starvation
By Allison Determan

When you are twenty years old, you look at yourself in the mirror. You are hungry. At twenty years old, you are always hungry. It is not a metaphorical hunger.

Since middle school, you've known that if you stop eating for long enough, your stomach will digest itself, crumple inwards into its own acid, its slippery mucus your last ever meal. The idea of no longer having a stomach seems like a welcome respite.

You cannot think. You haven't been able to think for months, and nobody has noticed.

You are twenty years old, and you have never been loved. You have been fucked by men who nip at your neck like stray dogs, who shift you onto their laps before the movie has introduced all of its characters, who ask you if you feel good as they're pulling up their pants. At twenty years old, you already know that this is not the same as being loved.

You watch your friends being loved. As you lay on the floors of their rooms, you watch them do their makeup and you listen to their stories. Their men bring them flowers. Their men ask them how their day was and do not kiss them until they are finished answering. You are hungry. It is a metaphorical hunger.

You have read enough self-help books to know the first step to finding a fulfilling romantic relationship is to love yourself. You despise yourself in the same clinical way that you dissect the diseased lab rats, slicing each tendinous thought from your brain and splaying it on a cold metal tray for observation. Like the rats, they are disgusting but not uniquely so. Back when you could think, you used to joke that killing rats is like riding a bicycle. You only have to feel their neck go soft under your hands once before you know how to do it forever. You can't unlearn how to kill a rat. You can't forget how to be hungry.

Your lab director is also your professor, and he tells you that he prefers when you wear dresses. At twenty, you have taken a class in gender studies, and you are able to identify that this remark is a subtle form of sexual harassment. Your friends would likely recount this story over dinner, their men's hands rested supportively on their knees, scoffing at the idea that they would let themselves be told what to wear to work. You start wearing dresses.

You despise yourself in the same efficient way you clean the rat's cages, the ethanol scent stinging the soft hollows behind your eyes as you shove your fingers between the bars of the cage and wipe the gray sulci clean of excrement.

Your job isn't really to clean the rat cages. Everybody knows that a diseased rat's cage is never clean. Your job is to maintain appearances for the weak-stomached investors who inevitably ask whether the research is humane. You are not paid well, but you save quite a bit of money by not eating.

At twenty years old, you are not deluded. You know that starving does not make you more likely to be loved. In fact, it makes you awful. You're tired all the time. You are never on time for anything and you're horrifyingly boring when you finally do show up. You are a terrible employee. You know that the only reason you have a job at all is because you do not object to wearing dresses. If you could still think, you know you'd be ashamed of yourself.

Your friends start bringing their men to events without asking. It's more palatable to be furious at their presumptuousness than to be furious at the loneliness that is eating away at your already threadbare heart until it is riddled with moth holes. Either way, you are furious, until the hunger numbs even that.

At twenty years old, you show up over an hour late to one of your shifts and by the time you finish up with the rats, the only other person there is the lab director who is also your professor. He asks if you need to grab dinner. He says he is hungry. He says that he is starving. He does not make it sound like a date.

You wish that he just asked you for a blowjob. You are much more scared of the dinner.

You hold the word no in your mouth like it is blood and you are standing on a white carpet. You are trying to be a scientist, and you are sick of describing your pain in metaphors. You bite the inside of your cheek hard enough that the slimy fat splits under your molars and you taste copper.

You remember the slew of men that your mother brought home when you were a child. You remember how they did not bring her flowers or ask about her day. You remember hearing them fuck her long before you knew what fucking was, your mother's keening little yelps keeping you awake at night. By high school, you were already annoyed at how generic your mother's pain was; you wished she would suffer more interestingly. By twenty, you have read enough self-help books to know that if you were a mother, you would probably repeat the same cycle of generational trauma.

You haven't had your period in over a year, and you don't think it will come back.

One of the men in the lab tells you that women are biologically designed to get pregnant at thirteen years old. He cites a study that correlates neonatal health with the age of the mother. The study does not say that adolescent mothers have a higher chance of dying in childbirth, though this is also true. He tells you that it makes sense why old men want to date young women, evolutionarily speaking. The professor who is also your lab director says nothing.

You can't be upset because it's true. You are upset anyways. You swallow it down like ipecac and it tastes the same.

In high school, you used to be able to run. Your thinness was the freeing kind. When smoke tendrils from illicit bonfires curled into the air, and warm malt liquor was produced from the back of pickup trucks, you could cartwheel beneath the stars until you didn't know which way was up. You could jump double Dutch with the elementary school kids who you babysat, the smacking of your bare feet on concrete like applause. You could sit in on a college lecture and watch the secrets of the universe crack open on the blackboard like a soft-boiled egg, syrupy and golden and laid out for you to consume.

You don't eat eggs anymore.

When you are alone in your apartment, you chew the restaurant panini that your lab director bought you but then you spit it out and swallow water instead. Your stomach is sloshing and uncomfortable by the time you finish, but it will be gone tomorrow morning when you piss.

Your roommate brings a man over and through the paper-thin walls of your apartment, you can hear him asking her if she wants to be touched. You do not speak to her for a week. Every time you try to ask her how to be loved, your tongue gets trapped under papery tables of foods and their corresponding calorie counts. When you eat, you taste nothing but 12-point double-spaced Times New Roman font.

You remember the first time a man touched your body without asking. You were fourteen and it was summertime, and you were high. You weren't alone. It wasn't late. It wasn't even all the way dark. You had bought yourself a slice of pizza and gotten pineapple on top despite the fact that there are forty calories in a half-cup of diced pineapple chunks. You didn't know that yet. You didn't care.

He grabbed your ass as you walked past him. He told you not to ruin it with pizza. He was drunk and he was laughing, and you ran the four miles back to South Station without saying goodbye to your friends. You wouldn't be able to do that now. Muscle weighs twice as much as fat, so you've let yours atrophy.

Since high school, you've known that there are fifteen calories in an average load of semen. You open your mouth when your lab director inevitably asks, but you do not swallow. You do not know who you are punishing.

At twenty years old, you look at yourself in the mirror. You despise yourself. There is nothing clinical or efficient about it. There is nothing you can tell yourself that will staunch your hemorrhaging desire to be loved. There is nothing you can tell yourself that will change the fact that you are hungry and nobody has noticed.

You inject the rats with disease. You watch them as they wither away. You look down at your own veins.

Keats in Virginia
By Livy Burnett

after Amy Clampitt

The dogwoods huddle
between pines and poplars
     laced with cardinals,
kinglets, birds blue as the Hampstead sky.
Humidity hums around them
     like a common breath.

At dusk, does tuck into the trees;
rib-thin coyotes slink from the horizon, roaming
     like starving prophets;
moths flutter out their microscopic lives,
soft and white, leaden-eyed,
     enamored with death.

Flecks of light spark in the darkness.
Earth-born souls hover above the creek
     as above Bassenthwaite;
the stars here are as steadfast, the night as tender.
I wonder if I couldn't simply fold
     into its obsidian.

Selected Poems by Charity Gingerich

Superstition

> After *Beach Scene*, watercolor and gouache
> on off white wove paper
> by James Hamilton

Brigs approach in the center of the setting sun.
The foreground scene could be a baptism, or a murder.
Or a wedding gone awry. Perhaps a new baby
dressed to please, or disguise, coos in the crook of
a grandmother's arm. The sunset is half heavenly,
half ominous, nothing new there, but the people
strewn along the sand, some wading out earnestly,
are more covered by shadow than light. Unjustified
beliefs are as easily dismissed as scientific facts:
how long did the world remain flat, its inhabitants
pitching off its four corners like a quilt being shaken?

Garden within a Garden

After Woman with a Parasol in a Garden by Renoir

Eve was a kind of garden, the first mother
of the first garden, so every woman thereafter

became an *either/or*: fertile or barren, Leah
or Rachel, green thumb or black thumb.

In this pretty little wilderness of flowers,
the strolling woman is merely another

blossom, a purple dahlia rendered black
by the dazzling light. *Hortus* then, another

word for the tiny world of orange seedlings
and galaxies she carries, that perennial paradise.

The Red-Eye
By Eden Mecham

Years ago, when I was naïve and hopeful and still believed that the Prophet talked to God in a place called the Holy of Holies, I married a returned missionary in the Mormon temple in Bountiful, Utah. The sun bleached the sky white on our wedding day. The gold-plated statue of Angel Moroni shimmered and danced atop the pinnacle of the temple, and with his trumpet in hand, he seemed ready to bugle out a call of eternal love. God was good. I knew that if we followed His path, He would bless our union in this life and in the next.

I strived to be the perfect Mormon wife, one who cooked and cleaned and honored her husband as the head of the household. I tried to mold myself into the type of woman the Prophet extolled: obedient, loving, and forgiving. I spent my days reading scripture, slicing potatoes for casseroles, and vacuuming the lush green carpets of our apartment. My husband and I settled into a type of contentedness. We were, I believed, the perfect picture of domesticity. And then—out of nowhere—my husband became convinced I was having an affair.

I did everything I could to prove my innocence. I let my husband monitor my emails. He furiously deleted the notes from my male friends, which said things like "I haven't heard from you in a while. Everything okay?" Or simply, "Is he treating you well?" I soothed my husband's anger by taking him to bed. I gave up going out with my male friends in the hopes that he'd see my devotion. He was still unhappy. He even accused my best friend, Lilly, of stealing me away from him. Eventually, his jealousy bubbled over into bouts of verbal rage, dark spells that shook my faith and left me wondering where we'd gone wrong. I cried. I prayed. I tried to find my way back to God's path. When I got pregnant with our first child, I gave up going out altogether. Things seemed to improve. But in the end, I couldn't cope with domestic isolation. I wanted something more.

Four years after that bright day in Bountiful, I left my husband and my religion. When I told my mother about my choices, she cried, got on her knees, and prayed for her lost child. My father settled into a state of silent disapproval. My Mormon friends, who didn't believe in divorce, began to treat me like an infectious disease—as if my rampant convictions and open wounds would somehow defile them. And I became solely responsible for a fragile, fluttery creature: a two-year-old daughter, Sylvia.

I was determined to tackle parenthood with grace and compassion. I would only talk to my daughter in an adult voice. I would treat her as a person with valid feelings. I wouldn't use religious guilt as a method of control. I wouldn't let our lives be dictated by the Prophet or by any other man. Instead, I would remake myself into the likeness of Rebecca West, the professed feminist, activist, and journalist who braved Yugoslavia during

World War II for the sake of her research—only Sylvia would accompany me on all my journeys. We would be inseparable. I was to be the kind of travel-writing adventure mom that taught her child about life by exploring foreign lands. She would learn to bake in the brick ovens of Rome. She would learn to sing by chanting over Senegalese fire rings. She would learn about wind patterns from sailing across the Atlantic. The world would be our education. Our travels would reclaim the lost years I spent in faithful submission.

Four months after I signed the divorce papers, I'd saved up enough money from my new editing business to plan our first trip: a three-thousand-mile journey across the country to visit an old friend in Manhattan. I packed our bags and booked the red-eye flight out of Portland International. My first mistake.

***

It was close to midnight, two hours after our flight was scheduled to leave, and Sylvia and I were still sitting by our departure gate. I had tucked her gently into her Mickey Mouse blanket, hoping (despite the blaring lights and buzzing conversation) that she would settle into sleep. But just when her tiny, blue-veined eyelids closed, the loudspeaker crackled alive: "Attention passengers: Flight 253 to New York has been delayed another twenty minutes. We've determined that the maintenance issue cannot be fixed, and we have another jet on its way."

A moan rose from the collection of people slumped in faux leather-backed chairs, and Sylvia bolted upright. She wiggled out of her blanket, arching her back to signal she wanted to get down. As soon as I set her on the carpet, she began toddling down the aisle.

I sighed, grabbed her Mickey Mouse blanket, her Disney Princess coloring book, her mismatched crayons, her sippy cup, my peacoat, both our scarves, and the box of raisins she had been snacking on. I shoved them all into my oversized duffle bag and followed her into the hallway, leaving our rollaway suitcases at the end of the aisle where I could keep an eye on them. We made a game of counting the cracks in the floor until the announcer called us back to board.

When we settled into our seats on the plane—thankfully, we had a whole row to ourselves—I undid the top button on Sylvia's jeans, pulled off her boots, and handed her the Mickey Mouse blanket.

"Okay, honey. Time for bed."

"No! Want milk!"

"Sweetpea, we don't have any more milk. You drank it all. Remember?"

"Want milk!"

"How about water?"

"Milk!"

"Sylvia, I don't have any milk, so I am going to fill your special cup with water. Okay?"

After producing the sippy cup, I picked her up, and we made our way to the bathroom at the front—stopping the flow of boarders coming in the other direction. *Excuse me. Excuse me. Sorry. Excuse me.* A flight attendant wearing too much blue eye shadow glared at us. I shrugged apologetically. *Sorry.* I knew the flight would be much more pleasant for everyone if Sylvia had something in her sippy cup to soothe her.

We squeezed into the bathroom cubicle. The folding door pressed inward too quickly, clipping Sylvia's leg, which made her shriek in surprise. She broke into tears. I bounced her up and down on my hip to try to calm her. The space smelled like stale sweat and piss. The sink was papered with sodden towels. The light above us flickered, as if too exhausted to cast out the darkness fully. I could see how none of this scenario was comforting to a tired toddler who was up way past her bedtime. Placing my forehead against Sylvia's, I inhaled and exhaled, inhaled and exhaled—until her breathing matched mine, and she settled. I filled her sippy cup as quickly as I could and then exited again, falling in line behind the last of the boarding passengers. Finally, I wrestled her into the seatbelt so the plane could take off.

***

The only other time Sylvia had been on an airplane was when my ex-husband and I had flown to Florida for spring break. She had been an infant at the time, and she had slept the entire way in my husband's arms. My husband was not the type of man to help out much with things like diaper-changing, potty training, or bath time. He preferred to hole up with his engineering books, spending the greater part of his evening hours industriously, scrawling out spidery equations on the whiteboard that enveloped the long wall in our bedroom. But on that trip, he surprised me. When the plane reached cruising altitude, he volunteered to watch her. Before I could respond, he had swept her up, cradled her in his arms, walked up and down the aisle, and patted her back until she was lulled to sleep. I distinctly remember the looks on the other passengers' faces—how they lit up when the two of them passed, how they smiled, whispered, stole glances at me, and winked as if to say: "You are lucky to have a such an attentive husband and a precious baby girl." In that moment—such a brief moment—we were the perfect portrait of a loving family.

On the plane to Manhattan, I had assumed that Sylvia would be an obedient toddler and sleep in my arms as she had in her father's that day. But Sylvia was not in the mood to be held. I tried spreading out her blanket across the two open seats and laid her down on her back. She stayed still for exactly two minutes until the

97

person behind us decided to turn on his reading light, which was aimed directly at Sylvia's face. She sat up. I tried to coax her into other sleeping positions: on her side across the two seats, on her stomach, using my lap as a pillow, in the sitting position with her head against my shoulder. All to no avail.

"Having troubles getting her to sleep?" asked the man in the aisle across from me.

Obviously. I turned to look at him. His forehead was creviced, but he had young eyes. He was holding a worn copy of *Waiting for Snow in Havana* by Carlos Eire, a book that I had been tempted to buy many times at the bookstore, but since my reading list was already six pages long, single-spaced, in twelve-point Times New Roman font, I hadn't yet gotten to it.

"Yes. She's absolutely exhausted, but for some reason, she won't sleep." I smiled, hoping for some intelligent conversation to ease my fatigue. I noticed that his hands were rough like a carpenter's, and I wondered what his day job was, and why the book cover looked like it had been run through the washing machine. "Good book?"

"Yes. It's a beautiful memoir." His fingertips were as gray as burnt charcoal.

I meditated on what it would be like to have such hands wrapped around my waist, to feel their strength and pressure in the small of my back. A red blush sprouted up my neck and bloomed into my cheeks. How could I think of another man in this way already?

"What makes it beautiful?" I asked, to keep him talking, to keep the fantasy at bay.

Sylvia started kicking the chair in front of her. I put a firm hand across her shins and gave her a sharp look. She folded her legs beneath her and jut her chin out defiantly, which was very unlike her. But I knew she was struggling to process this new and uncomfortable situation on zero sleep. I sighed and turned back to the man.

He ran one of his fingertips along the spine thoughtfully. "The way the author describes social dislocation—it's haunting and it makes sense." He pulled the book into his chest then and locked eyes with me. "And it speaks to a loneliness that many of us feel."

I felt a stirring in my core. Was that a pickup line? I couldn't tell. My experience with flirtation had been minimal. Like every teen, I attempted flirting in high school, but I was horrible at it, swinging my hair over my shoulder every five seconds and tripping every time I tried to do my "sexy walk." Then I was engaged at nineteen and married just after my twentieth birthday. I had been a virgin on my wedding night. So was my husband. I always thought that if I had done things as the Prophet prescribed, then intimacy with my husband would be blissful. I believed that God would smile down on us and bind us together—as one—for time and all eternity.

But our coupling was less than heavenly. Sometimes, the only way my husband could come was if he slapped me across the face first. The sex was almost always rough. It hurt. It did not bring us closer. But I knew—or at least I hoped—that intimacy could be sweeter, that it could be a less lonely affair.

"I think I would like that book," I said softly.

I wanted to mention something about Rebecca West to him, something about how in her masterpiece, *Black Lamb and Gray Falcon*, she explored the clashes and tenuous relationships caused by having many ethnic groups living in the same region. Social dislocation, I wanted to say, could happen even to those who were never exiled from their homelands. It could happen to those born into a landscape of cultural confusion. It could happen to those born into a culture they did not identify with. It could happen to someone like me, who was cast out because I had chosen divorce and started on a pathway that did not include God. My freedom had come at a cost. I had been cut away like chaff and discarded. Like Carlos Eire, I was very far from home.

But I didn't say any of those things. I was afraid that if I named my pain, it would become a living, tangible creature that could shove me back into a dark state of powerlessness at any moment.

The passenger must have seen the desperate longing in my face because he extended the book toward me and said, "Read the back. See if you like it."

I was about to take it from him when my attention was broken by Sylvia, who started laughing hysterically.

She was now standing up on the seat and throwing raisins at the passengers in the row behind us. "Raining," she said. "I like rain!"

"Sylvia!" I yelled a bit too loudly. That was my second mistake. She startled and started crying.

I craned my neck to look over the back of the seat. "Sorry," I said. "I'm so sorry."

Luckily, I think they were too tired to care. They waved off the offense as if batting at a pesky fly. It was nearly 2 AM.

"I have to get this one to go to sleep," I said to the man, officially ending our conversation.

He retracted his book, setting it on his lap. "Try lying her down on the floor. There's plenty of room for her down there." He then retreated to the words on the page, which probably offered a far more intelligent dialogue than I could offer in my sleep-deprived state.

I took his advice and put Sylvia on a blanket on the floor by my feet. She stretched out her arms and started thrashing about dramatically, like an injured sparrow. I reasoned with her, I cajoled her, I pleaded for her to sleep. I even quietly sang a lullaby, choking down my embarrassment at my very off-key melody in the hopes it would calm her. Finally, around four in the morning, her tiny eyelids fluttered closed. She slept for a precious forty-five minutes before the plane started to descend into a snowy New York morning.

Despite my exhaustion, I did not sleep at all. I kept thinking about Rebecca West. She left her child behind on her journeys. Was it really the best choice to drag Sylvia all around the world? I tried to picture what all of my traveling would bring us. Would it bring us closer? Or would Sylvia hate me for it? Would she blame me for leaving her father? Would we ever find a place to call home? Were we fated to always feel displaced?

Far too soon, a tired voice crackled on the loudspeaker, announcing that we needed to prepare for landing. It was time to wake Sylvia.

"Honey," I said, shaking her shoulder gently, "we're landing. It's time to get back in your seat."

She lifted her head. Two parallel lines of red imprinted her cheek where her blanket had wrinkled under it. Her glazed eyes looked disoriented.

"Come on, sweetie." I lifted her into the seat and buckled her belt before she could protest. She started whimpering.

"Let's get you ready." I started putting on her boots without waiting for her acknowledgement. My third mistake.

She kicked violently. "No shoes!"

"Sylvia, it's really cold outside." I wrapped my arms around my shivering body to demonstrate. "Brrr! You need your boots," I said, reaching for her foot again.

"No shoes!" she screeched, arching her back, so her feet were out of my reach.

"Sylvia, I can't carry you. I have to carry two suitcases and your bag. And you can't go outside without boots, your feet will get all wet and cold."

"No shoes!" she yelled at the top of her lungs, kicking and thrashing against her seatbelt, her wails reaching a tantrum pitch.

I quickly realized that I could not rationalize with a two-year-old who had only had forty-five minutes of sleep. So, I did what any good mother would do next: I started threatening her.

"Sylvia, if you don't stop crying this instant and put on your shoes, you're going in time out!"

This, of course, led to more crying and kicking. She could not be convinced.

The man across the aisle from us shifted uncomfortably in his seat. He put his book away, grabbed his iPod and headphones out of his backpack, and distinctly turned away from us. Even though I hadn't been seeking his approval, his sudden indifference to our situation troubled me. I tried to see myself through his eyes and the picture was not pretty: a frazzled, single mother who could not control her wildly ill-behaved child. Whatever connection we had over books and philosophy and social-cultural isolation had been effectively snuffed out by my inability to handle a tired toddler. I tried to quiet these thoughts by methodically tucking Sylvia's toys, blanket, and stray raisins back into her carry-on.

When we landed, Sylvia was still in full-on screaming-crying-writhing mode. I decided to wait out the tantrum. We were only a few rows back, so I sat there (trying to look calm) while nearly every passenger in the plane passed us to exit. Some laughed. Some shook their heads. Some said things like "Oh, poor thing!" or "I feel the same way." But most looked awkwardly in the other direction. The man next to us had left without as much as a backward glance.

Nothing had an effect on Sylvia. When the last passenger got off the plane, I tried again. "Okay, Sylvia. Everyone is off the plane. It's our turn now." I reached for her foot. She kicked me in the knee as hard as she could.

"Excuse me, Ma'am. You need to exit the plane, so we can clean it for the next flight." It was the woman with the heavy blue eye shadow again. What did she expect me to do? Toss Sylvia in the duffle bag along with the blanket?

I looked at her closely. The angry vertical crease between her eyebrows told me she meant business. "Just a minute," I said and turned to Sylvia again, making one last desperate attempt to put on her shoe by force. She flung it across the aisle.

"Ma'am…"

"Just a minute."

"Ma'am, you have to leave the plane NOW."

The other two flight attendants came up behind her to stare at us open-mouthed. I wondered if any of them had ever had kids. I was suddenly aware that we were a spectacle to them—like a grotesquely fascinating sideshow—and an easy target for their judgment.

"Fine," I said wearily. They all watched as I retrieved her boots. They all watched as I pulled one heavy rollaway down from the overhead bin and then the next, placing them in the aisle. They all watched as I flung the duffle bag over one shoulder, picked up the thrashing two-year-old with the crook of my arm, and awkwardly grabbed the first rollaway with the three fingers I had available on that hand. They all watched as I dragged the second suitcase behind me and headed onto the jet bridge. No one offered to help. No one offered a kind word.

The suitcase in front of me knocked against my ankles, Sylvia kicked at one hip, the duffle bag bumped against the other, while the suitcase behind me veered every which way. I could feel bruises forming where Sylvia's small ankles connected with my leg, but I kept walking. I kept walking and walking. One foot in front of the other. It was the only thing to do.

When we finally made it inside the airport, Sylvia yanked my hair and I dropped everything, including her. Her wails changed from those of distress to those of shock. "Mamma drop me!" she accused.

At that point, my rational brain stopped working, and I flung myself to the ground beside my child and started crying too. Not just little sniffles, but loud, outright, back-shaking sobs.

I was sobbing smack dab in the middle of La Guardia airport.

But I wasn't just crying because I was frustrated and exhausted. I was crying because for the first time, I truly realized how alone I was in the world. I suddenly missed my ex-husband. I mean, I really missed *him*, not just his extra set of arms. I missed the way he absent-mindedly tickled the back of my neck while he read about fluid mechanics and jet propulsion. I missed the way his ears turned red when he laughed too hard. I missed the way he turned his body into a human motorcycle and allowed Sylvia to "drive" him around the living room floor. I didn't want him back—that was for certain. Our marriage had been toxic and suffocating. He wanted a diligent Mormon housewife who only left the house to attend homemaking meetings on Wednesdays and church on Sundays. I wanted to scatter my fingerprints in foreign places, make my mark.

But, for a brief moment, I wished he was still in our lives. I wished we could have had held onto that picture-perfect moment in the airplane bound for Florida. Why wasn't he there to pick us both back up? Why couldn't he have been our home?

At the same time, I was mad at myself for needing him. Rebecca West started her career husband-free. She had a lover, for a time, and bore a child. But she never let motherhood hold her back. She traveled extensively, censured communism, fought savagely for women's rights, and published her work in *The Times, New Republic,* and *The New Yorker.* In 1947, in an age when women were not considered able correspondents, *Time* announced that she was "indisputably the world's number one woman writer." How was I ever to become a Rebecca West, with her vigilante take-life-by-the-balls attitude, if I couldn't even handle a two-year-old on my own?

Finally, a wide-hipped woman from the service counter approached us. "Oh, honey. Can I help you? What seems to be the problem?"

I lifted a limp, battered Tinker Bell boot from the duffle bag and held it out to her. "She won't…put on…her boots," I said between sobs.

"Well, let's see what we can do about that." She took the boot and smiled at Sylvia. "And what's your name, cutie?"

My daughter paused her crying to look the stranger up and down. "Sylvia."

"That's a beautiful name!"

The flattery made Sylvia forget her grief, and she offered the lady a few hiccups and a shy smile.

"Sylvia, do you think we could put on your shoes now?"

She lifted each foot sheepishly, so the nice woman could put on her boots.

The woman went to work, and a moment later, Sylvia was tear-free and outfitted. It took me a little longer to stop crying, but I finally got there, profusely thanking the airline employee for her help.

I made a lot of mistakes that day. But as I reorganized the baggage and helped Sylvia adjust her coat, I began to break down the walls of my illusions. My life would never be picture-perfect because I was not perfect. I was not a perfect Mormon wife, neither was I destined to be a perfect Rebecca West. My life as an independent woman and a single parent were going to be uniquely my own. Some days would come close to my ideal vision. I would travel with Sylvia to many domestic and foreign destinations: we'd sew textiles in the woolen mills of Ireland; we'd dive into building-high waves on a beach in the West Indies; we'd fashion hiking sticks out of fallen branches in the Canadian Rockies. I would learn what it felt like to have a generous and gentle lover. Eventually, I'd marry again. But most days were going to be long and lonely and frustrating.

Outside the airport, the snow was swinging in short, powerful bursts. The sidewalk was slushed with thousands of footprints. The taxi line curled around the corner. Men and women—strangers—huddled into each other, their suitcases stacked haphazardly.

I dragged our luggage to the end of the line with Sylvia toddling behind. Flurries of snow beat against our coats and blew into our open eyes.

"Mamma, I cold," she said.

I situated our bags behind the last person in line, picked her up, and wrapped her into my body. "Don't worry. Mommy will keep you warm," I said.

And we stood there, the two of us, waiting for what was to come.

Selected Poems by Sarah Kersey

The Choreography of Geese

The geese are okay
being codependent vagabonds.

Together, they form an arrow
pointing to Florida with no feathers

ruffled, no broken song, no objections
or second guesses littering flight.

The birds simply fall in line, practicing blind
reliance, assuming the bird in front knows

what shape to make in the clouds, trusting
they will stop before flying into fire, even

though we are all trying to get warm.
How human to seek togetherness

in a frozen world. How animalistic.
If we were geese, I would have followed

you into the sun.

Blush Portrait (In Pink)

In this portrait of myself, I correct the rendition
of my dimples: not hollow enough. They should
be craters, concave and collapsing, folding in
on themselves. Memory's echo does not grant
me the gift of forgetting your fascination
with the absences cowering under my
blush, your stern index finger nesting
in the pink pothole of my cheek,
your fingerprint like a bad face
tattoo, the time you told me
what a shame it was my cheeks
produced caves with no diamonds.
Eight years later I find you, and with your eyes
on my face, the mines in mine collapse. I look
in the mirror that night and do not have the luxury
of forgetting how I used to say *thank you.*

slice of life
By Ela Kini

amma doesn't remember *appa*'s palm held in hers.
when I was still soft as the womb intended,
      she called his fingers a whisper
      that she held beneath her ribs.
amma said a person was their fingers,
that fingers know body how heart never will.
      and in winter, *appa* tugs in stitched burlap sacks
      brimming with rice between covered hands.
cold glazes him, a varnish. snow stiffens his coat.
he pulls away his mittens, traces *amma*'s fingers
      across his bare palms.
      they indulge in the heat of fire
until their hands are warm and bound together,
roots stitching into soil.
      when he pulls his hand away,
      amma forgets it again,
remembers only snow pattering windows.
at noon, they sip tea and swallow too-ripe grapes,
      think of the fruit as their own bodies.
      appa gives her a fig,
tells her it is aged as his fingertips.
she bites into the flesh, tracing the skin,
      body moving carefully,
      practicing the art of caressing memory.
I ask what the fruit tastes of and wait
for an answer which doesn't come
         and she simply smiles
         until their bodies are full.
they sit until evening, trading palms.
amma remembers her hand smooth
      as the waxy skin of apples.
      when *appa* carves these,
he peels away the red coat for compost or rebirth,

then draws brisque slices through the body,
        not letting juice spill over the countertop.
        amma holds a slice to her teeth, nibbles
at youth. when night falls and the fire's scraps
of log are charred, her eyes close.
        appa murmurs psalms to the open night as if
        they are ours. spills his fingers across the pages.
amma's hands once drew through this book
with ritual ease, each cover an extension of her
                waking and resting body.
                we never believed but *amma* did, in life
        mirroring the words written.
        so, he paused as his tongue fell across *memory*
and each of the fruits the passages named,
figs and pomegranates they once cut together.
        each word pressed against his palette,
        heavy as whisper and quiet as breath.
                when his eyes fell across the last page,
                he placed back the bound stories.
he washed the cutting knives
between calluses and fell into sleep,
        dragging *amma*'s fingers
across his beating chest, their hands clasped.

Appetite of an Eldest Daughter
By Levi Abadilla

i.

When Mother mourns her turbulent childhood, you bottle her tears
like the obedient and caring daughter you are. You are supposed to.
Who else is going to know her sorrow? She suffered a childhood
you should be thankful she will not give you, and so the least you
can do is take all that hurt and be grateful for her mercy (that's what
she says, anyway). So you learn, as all daughters should, how to
catch her misery just right, in a way that none of it spills and burns
your tender skin.

ii.

Mother loves you so she feeds you all the things a growing daughter
needs: *those clothes look awful, should you really be wearing that?*
your hair looks so nice, don't cut it short or let it grow too long. I
don't like your friends, find better ones. have you been keeping your
grades up or are you spending all your time on that silly shit?

  She doesn't curse, of course (she's a mother!), but you know
the taste of the things she doesn't want to hear from your mouth.
You mumble them under your breath when she's not looking, bark it
out in laughter when you're with people she'd throw a fit over
seeing you hang out with. Rebellion tastes sharp and electric on the
teenage tongue, still fresh and new to your discovering senses. You

devour it with the fascination of the curious and kiss people she doesn't want you to be kissing behind decrepit buildings. When she knowingly asks you why you're home late, you ask her what she's talking about.

iii.

Mother slides you her favorite foods every breakfast and dinner. You've seen them in her childhood photos, and your only reprieve from them is when you grab lunch elsewhere. When you were younger, you dutifully chewed and drank and swallowed, because what else were you supposed to do? When you ask for something else now, your mother cries, because how could you say that to her? So you chew and drink and swallow and spit everything you can't stomach into the toilet, and the crevices of your room fill with everything your mother would never let you put between your teeth.

The sharp and electric taste of once-new rebellions are now dull and tired to your growing palate, so you're chasing new recipes for excitement, finding new adventures that get your stomach flipping. In your young mind, it's unfair that Mother knows everything the world has to offer, but insists on keeping you bird-fed, chewing worms before pouring it down your should-be-grateful throat. You are tired of worms. You are tired of bird-feeding. Mother tells you if you fly around without her, you will swoop down at the wrong time and smash into pink and red and yellow against the glass of a speeding car's windshield.

iv.

You are Mother's pride and joy, because she wants you to be intelligent, she wants you to be confident, and she wants you to be perfect. *Wants you* is being generous, of course—you *should be* intelligent, you *should be* confident, you *should be* perfect. You are, after all, your mother's daughter. You look in the mirror and inspect your bony face, your pock-marked skin, and your too-wide shoulders. Mother says there is fat in places there shouldn't be *(because you don't eat what I tell you to)* and your ribs are poking through your skin *(because you eat things I tell you not to)*. You step on the weighing scale, and you can't see the numbers, just hear Mother tut *too much, too fat, too thin, too little.*

She sits you down and writes a whole menu of the things that will fix you. It is the same things she has been feeding you forever, because you are a stubborn, selfish, stupid long-time project, and you've made her spend all these years trying to fix you. She loves you, of course, and she is your mother, so she will make the sacrifice. You should listen this time. You should be grateful. Maybe then there wouldn't be so much to fix. Don't be silly, you're never going to be perfect. Just tolerable. You are your mother's child.

v.

Everyone is responsible for the suffering of your mother: her family, her own mother, your father, and in some capacity, you. She's had an eventful and troubled life, if you can even call what pockets she had when she wasn't going through the motions of surviving as *living*. She didn't want to be raised by a cruel mother. Once, you asked her if she wanted to marry your father, and she didn't answer. You moved on and asked if she wanted you and your siblings, and she just looked at you. You thank God every day that she didn't answer you because it's one thing to know she didn't want any of you and another thing entirely to hear it from her. Maybe in another world, you don't exist, and she gets more control over her life. Maybe in another world, she's free.

You don't want to be like her. You want to have control over your life. You want to fight. You want to shape your future with your own hands and with as much authenticity as possible.

And your mother must have once wanted all of that too.

When you were younger, she existed as a permanently fully-formed concept in your mind, one with no origin point or endpoint. She had always been there, was always right, and could shift the world a certain way if she wanted to; the easiest your mind could personify God. Now older, you realize your mother must have hidden things she shouldn't have in the crevices of her bedroom too, looked in the mirror and listened to *too much, too fat, too thin, too little*. History writes itself into tree rings, stress robs the taste of meat, mothers pass their cravings onto their children.

In another life, you don't exist, and she doesn't have to run from the ghost of her own mother every time she looks at you. In another life, maybe she's happier—or maybe she's just sipping on another flavor of misery. Life loves variety with the same damn drinks. When you grow up, maybe you'll pretend to be better than her, and your eldest will trade smoke rings in parking lots and kiss people they shouldn't be kissing.

vi.

You love your mother. You hate her. No, hate is a strong word, so perhaps *resent* would be better. She made you everything you are; she made you everything you didn't want to be. You wouldn't be here without her; you don't want to be where you are now. You know all her greatest fears and worst years; she gave you your greatest fears and worst years. When she looks at herself in the mirror, she sees you; when you look at yourself in the mirror, you see her.

You both hate it—no, hate is a strong word. You love your mother, in the same way she says she loves you.

vi.

When you leave home, she cries and cries and cries, and you don't know if it's because she's finally free or because you're leaving her in the house with your father. You're taking your siblings, because they begged you to, and even if they didn't, you wouldn't be able to sleep at night knowing you're out of that house, but they aren't.

Your mother tells you to call and drop by every now and then, and you tersely nod and say *sure, okay, if I have time, if I'm not too busy.*

You have a new phone with a fresh, empty contacts list. You will ask your friends and your siblings for their numbers later, and if hers doesn't join theirs, then you must have forgotten. What a tragedy.

She invites (insists, with that clipped, raised voice you associate with slammed doors and shattering glass) you for one last lunch, and you agree just so she doesn't have a reason to hunt down your address and show up uninvited. You both sit across from each other on the kitchen island, staring down at your own cups of lavender tea. Your mother sips hers, and you stare at yours. You are allergic to lavender tea, you've told her this several times. You don't know if she didn't hear you or if she's just ignoring it. Or if she's old and her memory's not as well as it used to be. You're older now. You want to give her the grace and sympathy she didn't give you, even if she doesn't deserve it. In the last few years, you've realized it's easier to stop trying to figure out how she works.

She reminds you to keep your house in order and to stop wasting your time and life. You ask her if she's fine being by herself with your dad. She doesn't answer. You push your cup of tea away, careful not to splash any on your skin.

"I don't know where I went wrong with raising you," she says with so much grief that for a moment you think she cares. But if you entertain the thought for too long, you might stay in the house for another night, and no matter how much you see your face in the lines of your mother's, you know it's better for both of you to go your separate ways. This is her *another life.* This is as close as non-existence you can gift her. One last act of affection for a woman whose love you don't understand.

"I don't know why you hate me so much."

"I don't hate you."

You stand up and grab your bags. You've indulged her already, that should be enough. You don't wave goodbye as you step out of the door.

You wonder if all the things she did back then were her trying to take control of her life. If she wanted to shape the future with her hands, through you and at the cost of you. You wonder if you're doing the same thing as you're leaving her.

In the house, you hear her crying. You don't look back. You *are* your mother's daughter.

Selected Poems by Isabel Gan

elegy for the weeping willow and daffodils

it seems strange to think—that i should grieve their blooming.

they bloom in spring, after all; it is the season of hope
and rebirth. yet i watch as raindrops run down the leaves
of the weeping willow, and think—it is so aptly named
for its perpetual misery. listen closely; hear it weep for its
own misery and that of those whom it casts its looming
shadow upon. back then, the willow softly crooned the death
of alexander the great, its tendril-like leaves sweeping his
glorious macedonian crown back to the earth's womb
as he crossed the euphrates in presumptuous triumph.
on the island of saint helena, its pendulous branches guard
the burial site of napoleon, brushing over his cancer-stricken body
in callous consolation. surely, the willow knows that its
gracefully rounded crown is but a crude mockery of
napoleon's disgrace.

rooted along the riverbank, daffodils forever bear the scars
of a handsome youth wasting away, lustful eyes still fixed
upon the silvery waters. within the ripples, a face smiled
back at him—strangely, enchantingly, hauntingly familiar.
as he whispered his devotion, a raspy rustle in the wind
echoed it back, unheard. as the youth wasted away he beat
against his bronze-sculpted chest, bruised and battered, from
whence grew the daffodil—borne out of the barren soil
of a selfish heart. hence the narcissi are stark yellow
for the golden radiance of his hair, deep purple for the
brokenness of his once-loved body.

and so i grieve as they bloom—for their blooming marks demise.
in the daffodil is the death of youth, the loss of self against the
tumultuous vicissitudes of life. and in the weeping willow

it is revealed—the mortality of man cannot prevail;
hubris is man's fail.

self-portrait in perdendosi

perdendosi—(adj.)
/per·den·do·si -dō͵sē/
[from Italian, perdendo meaning
to disappear, to lose itself, to vanish]
used as a direction in music where
the sound gradually / dies away.

i tune my voice to fit the melody that
society wants me to sing / just like the lyrical
lyrebird, i have mastered mindless mimicry
of herd mentality, an instrument / silencing those
who modulate and refuse blind conformity—
if deviation is a sin / i confess my innocence.

i close my eyes and sing the same melody
she sings / but she sings the same melody
he sings / but he sings the same melody
i sing / all of us too quietly afraid to diverge
and start a different melody // so begins
a cyclical ostinato of self-suppression.

all souls are made different / yet we choose
to be the same / i find that i am no different from
the norm // the *liar*-bird sings as i repress my
individuality and self-concept / my traitorous
heart cries out to be unfettered / realize that in
the end, we are no different from caged birds.

slowly, i lose myself / as i watch her slowly
lose herself / as she watches him slowly
lose himself / as he watches me slowly

lose myself // slit the lyrebird's throat; watch
me dissipate, *perdendosi* as the direction of my
ostinato (melody) / dying away

into nothingness.

Landlocked
By Audrey Towns

Cumulus waves crest overhead, darkening
dry sand, shadowed glaciers drifting
at her feet. Their peaks break her rotting
resignation with pockets of nostalgia and pleasure.

She shows me photos of her wild windswept
hair in front of lavish resorts, wrapped porches
painted in vibrant reds, yellows, and greens,
dreamcatchers and blue glass bottles
perched in the openings where well-known faces
and well-off families roosted in summer months.
Street signs with names like
Honolulu and Acapulco Avenue promised paradise,
sun-soaked bodies and jeweled necks
glittering at the seaside clubs,
enjoying perfectly plated filets
fresh from the Salton Sea.

Nothing now remains
in the residue of those receding dreams,
but toxic dust basking on the beaches,
shifting shorelines into graveyards
in the suffocating salt.
Her lungs and life hang heavy, mummified,
left to sink in stagnant rust-colored pools,
where breath and buildings move in raspy heaves,
waiting for waves to return
and wet her weathered skin.

We stand on a vast swath of lakebed
looking at lonely skeletons
of tilapia and wintery trees searing in salt snow.
She thinks of her own bones
crunching each morning
in the brackish air as she
reluctantly rises from bed.

I see her eyes still following the clouds,
their soft fleeting forms gathering water,
the only escape from
a sea with no outlet,

unless air, or economy,
can lift you.

Circle of Animals
By Deanna Whitlow

It came forth unceremoniously, like a shattering. I was only supposed to be home for a weekend, to maybe say goodbye to the house and the neighbors and the ocean, but when they saw me, all bones again, they wouldn't let me leave. Half of California had burned down just before my parents were set to move to Texas. Mom kept the group text updated when the fires were raging, asking me and my brother if there was anything in particular we wanted her to save if they had to evacuate. I imagined my bedroom from my Chicago apartment and asked her to take my copy of *On Beauty* by Zadie Smith and my first pair of pointe shoes. Our distant suburbia had survived although the lemon trees had gone pallid and droopy. Neighborhoods like ours that were spared were dusted with a dense layer of ash and the air, even months later, still smelled of charred pine and smoke.

The fires were not the reason for moving. It was just the natural order of things. And I knew my parents were not happy about moving again, especially to Texas. They grew up there. I didn't learn the whole stories of their respective strange and traumatic childhoods until we got there, and the roads and people and sky of their history drew it out of them. It made it easy to understand why they found it easier to love their home from a distance.

From the time they left Texas in the early 90s, they moved every one to three years. That made thirteen moves for them, eleven for my brother, and ten for me. We had done it so many times that it typically happened with minimal sentimentality and an almost scientific precision. Our things would be layered in boxes, wrapped in plastic, and transferred to somewhere new where we'd follow around a veneer-clad real estate agent to search for a new, albeit temporary, home. I didn't hate moving until I hit adolescence and became embarrassed of everything: my skin, my body, my unrootedness.

This was the first move I would not be in the middle of and—although Chicago felt lonely, and I was starving myself again—I felt the fleeting relief of gratitude. *I get to be rooted here* I thought as I jogged along the perimeter of Lake Michigan.

***

It was around this time, too, that I became deeply troubled by the state of my birth chart. I would distract myself from hunger by researching my astrological fate. I did not like what I found. My chart lacks exaltation, it lacks ease. It is so much air trapped beneath rigid, unshakeable earth, leaving me no choice but to pollute the only real home I have. In my self-absorbed, delirious fervor I briefly considered that the universe might have found me insufferable until I remembered that I was nothing in the grand scheme of things.

Before I accepted that it was just something fundamentally flawed about the way I perceived my position in the world, I was convinced that moving was the reason for everything wrong with me. This was confirmed by the doctors and therapists and counselors who had no issue blaming my distorted self-perception on all the moving. *Your environment is unsettled*, they'd say. *So you search for control elsewhere.* I always thought that was a strange sentiment, that I try to forge home from self-destruction. They always failed to consider what it was like to be Black in these very white spaces, what it was like to be unavoidably visible no matter how much I tried to waste away.

***

So, it was November, and as the rest of the world was darkening and shriveling and preparing for winter, California lived on in perpetual bloom. White bushels of jasmine, orange Birds of Paradise, pink cactus flowers, the bluest skies and the greenest grass. Even through the leftover smog, it all was painstakingly vibrant. The thirty-mile drive from LAX to Agoura Hills took almost two hours with traffic. My mom prayed. Silently at first, but then out loud.

Protect her, oh God.

I hadn't thought of God in months.

Show her your grace.

God, or at least the version we make of him, is much kinder than the universe.

Heal her body, mind, and soul.

The stars and planets are predictable and unchanging. At least God has the propensity for movement, at least He can decide one day that he is not obligated to create suffering.

Mom started speaking in tongues and I let it lull me off to sleep.

***

In my astrological research, I learned that *zodiac* means *circle of little animals*. I remember making note of this because I found the image so beautiful and so strange, a smattering of animals aligning themselves to contain the universe.

***

The house was the second one from the corner. It looked like all the others—tan stucco and brick with a tall palm tree peeking out from the backyard and a Crape Myrtle tree that left brigades of pink flowers behind. We, however, did not fly the American flag like the rest of the neighborhood did. And my parents had the white door painted a deep, chestnut brown. When it swung open it was like the opening of a void. I stepped inside.

They must have left the house frantically because they had forgotten to blow out one of the candles. It was burning angrily, nearing the bottom of the wick. It had only been a week or two since they found out they were moving, so they had not started arranging the house for showings and walk-throughs. This was the last time, though, I'd see it looking like ours. Before we'd take all of the family photographs down in case potential buyers were racist. Before shifting the coffee table in the living room over a few feet to cover the slightly faded spot where my old dog used to go around and around before he had the courage to lay down to rest. Way before everything was in boxes and way before the house was empty. It was still home, and it was all so beautiful. But I wanted to be anywhere else.

***

We moved to California during a heatwave. It was the summer before my senior year of high school and for the first week of July, the temperature scraped 108 degrees almost every day. We had not found the house yet, so we were staying in the tiny, unairconditioned guest house of one of my dad's work friends. It felt like standing at the gates of hell. I briefly considered that God might be punishing me for my adolescent stint with atheism until I remembered that I was nothing in the grand scheme of things.

When it cooled, though, when a tiny mist of rain marked the end of the drought and what was dead tried to force itself back to life, I started to see the beauty of Los Angeles that they are always writing songs about. It's the isolation, I think, that is so romantic. When you are in California, it feels like you are in a separate world. There could be a snowstorm on the other side of the country without you receiving even a referential gust of cold air. Everything grows there. It is beautifully relentless.

***

Mom told me I had a doctor's appointment at 11:30 AM, but that I had to eat something beforehand. I picked up an apple from the fruit bowl and examined the sticker. It was a McIntosh apple, like I'd expected. It was still the only kind they bought—a practice leftover from our years in Connecticut where the reddening of leaves meant the orchards would be open. I moved to run the apple under the tap when Mom told me I needed something more substantial. She rummaged through the pantry as I sat at the table. She sat next to me, between me and my dad, and started spreading a thin layer of avocado on a piece of sourdough bread.

Over the ten moves across ten states, I had never seen my parents love a place like they loved California. This was the only time I saw them change for a place. They had never lost their southerness until here, where they traded in grits and bacon for avocado toast and strawberries from the fruit stand down the street. Where they replaced white sugar and powdered creamer in their coffee for vanilla almond milk or honey harvested in Ojai. They suddenly only drank orange juice when they could make it fresh from the citrus tree in the backyard. They had changed and they were radiant. I liked this version of home more than all of the others.

***

The doctor's appointment was uneventful. They drew blood. They weighed me and it was a bad number, but the back of my eyes glowed with excitement. They told me my heart rate was dangerously low and that any intense exercise could put me at risk of a heart attack. They told my mom to watch me and make sure that I wasn't doing any intense exercise, so before we left, I did a hundred jumping jacks in the bathroom.

***

Here's how it goes when it comes to my astrological makeup. Sun in Libra, represented by the scales (ironic), is the only inanimate object within the circle of animals. It makes me a people pleaser with a tendency towards vanity. My moon is in detriment in Capricorn, which apparently means I seek discomfort and my Venus in Virgo in the twelfth house makes it so I can only love what is perfect.

***

When we got back to the house, Dad said I should stay with them for a while. *Then once we settle in Texas, we can find a facility nearby.*

I said okay although I would have rather died than waste three months in a hospital. I was still unaware of the gravity of my physical state and could only think about school and how if I had to take a semester off during my undergraduate program, I would not be able to finish my MFA before twenty-five, meaning I would not have a chance of finishing a novel before twenty-six, so would not be able to publish before twenty-eight, and all of this seemed a fate worse than death or incapacitation or constant, ravenous, hunger. I also said okay because I could tell that they were afraid.

***

It's still a little smoggy around here, my dad said and grabbed the keys off the table. *We should go get some fresh air.*

Our neighbors from a few doors down were walking by as we approached our car. Their house also looked like ours, except for during the election when they flew a "Make America Great Again" flag like they were preparing to wage war. And they were nice people if you ignored their Facebook posts about "all lives matter" and the microchip vaccine. They started making small talk about the move. We smiled politely and nodded along.

"We might be following close behind to Texas," the man said. He wore cargo shorts year-round and had a "Don't tread on me" sticker on his Ford Escape. "I'm about tired of Governor Newsom and his woke shit."

"We actually really love it here." Mom was trying to cut the conversation short. "We're going to miss it."

"Well," the woman said. She was a victim of the luxury athleticwear, Botox, and hair bleach cult. Her face barely moved as she spoke. "We sure are going to miss you all. You know, you were surprisingly good neighbors."

I liked this version of home less than all of the others.

***

I am thinking of the circle of animals again and what it means to be surrounded. You can be surrounded in a home by the walls that stand, you can be surrounded in a prison by concrete and metal bars.

By hands reaching towards your neck or arms opening to hold you in an embrace. To be surrounded is to be simultaneously comforted and threatened by your inability to escape.

***

The California suburbs are a sort of surrounding. They are so deceptively peaceful until it is easy to forget that the wilderness of the ocean thrashes only a few miles away. There are small reminders in the occasional briny salt breeze traveling further than normal or when a seagull takes a wrong turn and ends up perched on your mailbox. Sometimes even in the strength of the moon's light or the neon cobalt of a clear sky. We drove in silence except for the gospel music streaming softly from the radio. The ocean is another type of surrounding. It can drown you or baptize you in one fell swoop.

The waves broke through first, always. Easing around the bend of a cliff, the lapping chorus of the tides joined the hum of cars on pavement and rustling leaves. I let down my window and took a deep inhale. The air is different. It is clean like it has never been processed before, like each breath is a new one that no one else has ever taken. Then, the horizon lowers, the cliffs taper off, and the ocean is there, crawling forth like a hungry animal from its hole. It shimmers like the cup of trembling, like an empty house scrubbed clean of life.

Selected Poems by Mike Bove

Deep Winter Survival

My son calls out in sleep, some sudden cry
inside a dream, and the house, still

at this hour, and dark, holds his sound
overhead, me in bed on my back

the next room over. How many creatures,
mice or foxes, move around us just outside?

How many bare limbs and fallen leaves
lay marooned on the lawn under snow?

He confessed he'd gotten good at listening
in school. Each time there was an unexpected

noise, fallen book or windblown door,
he heard it as gunfire and froze beneath its blast.

Cold, these nights. Dark, those creatures
on the lawn. What could I tell him about

sound, about newsfeed-anxiety
and lockdown drills? Helpless and hungry,

I crave an ending. Even asleep, something
inside him wants out, needs bursting,

expulsion into night. Let me devour
his fear. I'm begging, starving

like desperate foxes searching the snow.

I'll eat that sound and all that made it,

gulp it like a stone of ice, wishing
it would melt, worried it won't.

In December We Talk

about how different the light is
during winter months, slanted
and freshly sharp. You often
tell me your marriage is in peril.
It never is. I often say my kids
are in trouble. They always
pull through. Things feel
precarious in raw times.
Look at these islands, this ocean
we pass on chilly afternoons.
It's easy to imagine we won't
survive cold coastal months,
but it's just not true. There
a gull is rising. And there
the sand where no ice forms.
A frozen beach rose
we've passed a hundred times.
In four months it will drip color.
We'll believe nothing ever dies.

Hospice
By Kaley Hutter

Your hands slide into the
          sidling soil—laundered copper plunged into
the mouth of the earth.

It kisses the lines on your knuckles like rings,
          sucks down the seeds
you toss it. You toss your head

back, and the magnolia trees curl
          around your bricked kingdom like pet dragons.
As a child I coaxed the dead-

heads from the ground's brown throat.
          They balked, bore my pink-thumbed grip,
begged and breathed for your wrinkled warmth.

          On the day you stop breathing, the ground knows it first.

I drive in from New York to the room
          they slid you in,
your hair wilted and hands braided

in expired prayer and dried sap,
          the same syrups that sling between all those stars,
and *here is what I imagine*

the hydrangeas in heaven will look like   is what I say.
          But you have gleaned the land naked,

your earthen eyes already fixed

on the winged magnolias at the edge of this property,
      who too have known
the mouth of the earth.

Everything they taught us about horticulture is a lie.
By S Maxfield

"Peonies are indecent, Margaret."

This is Sister Verena's answer when I ask if we can plant them in the tiny plot we're weeding near the school entrance. I add *peonies* to my mental List of Impure Desires. A bushel blooms in my mind surrounding another entry: *Stephanie*. I should have known that such delicately soft, beautifully round, delightfully opulent flowers were off-limits. Stephanie's swirls of curls wave in the breeze of my thoughts. I should have known. Sister Verena smacks my shoulder, and points me to another cluster of dandelions.

I first saw peonies in a seed catalogue at Wal-Mart. My dad had asked the clerk for advice about grass as an excuse to brag about our lawn: *Tall fescue is the future!* I flopped down on the patio display set and flipped through the sample catalogue. There, between the unassuming pansies and everyday petunias was: PEONY. I stopped breathing. What kind of person has *this* in their yard? (Apparently: the kind of person who conjures objects, thinks too much about Stephanie Hannaham, and is definitely going to Hell.) *Conjuring* is also on my List.

We have been weeding for an hour, and my hands are blistered. Sweat pools at my armpits. Dirt smudges the knees of my tights. My banana clip has slid fully sideways, as I battle a particularly stubborn weed. And now (of course) Stephanie walks by. She's with Jamie from my history class, who waves, calling, "Hey, Meg!"

I wave back and try, unsuccessfully, to sink into the upturned earth. Stephanie smiles.

Stephanie Hannaham smiles, and a thousand peonies bloom. My mind is a riot of dazzling, pastel color exploding in all directions. Then she and Jamie disappear around the corner, and I'm just kneeling in the dirt with a handful of dead dandelions.

Sister Verena sends me home for dinner. I sneak in the side door and try to get most of the mud off my tights before putting them in the laundry. There's dinner and homework, like always. My parents argue over the dishwashing, like always. I'm brushing my teeth. I see my face in the mirror and wonder: What does *Stephanie* see when *I* smile? And then I spit into the sink, trying to rinse my thoughts away with the toothpaste.

I sit on my bed holding Abracadabra, the bear my aunt gave me when I was three. I tell him about the peonies. His faded embroidered eyes are unfazed, expressing no judgment. He already knows about the rest of the List: *Stephanie, conjuring, cigarettes, everything.* I ask him if he thinks it's okay to practice conjuring if I say ten *Hail Marys* after. He doesn't respond. I take out my small box of paper clips and transform them one by one into a garden. Peonies.

The next day is Saturday, which means I'm reshelving at the library. I rake up scattered piles of picture books and periodicals, and then—*oh!* On an otherwise empty table, there's an oversized, full-color gardening book, opened to a two-page spread of peonies.

I look over my shoulder. I inch near the table and peek. I sit down and stare. I want to cry. They are so abundant, so impossible. I hear footsteps and hastily close the book, shoving it onto my cart.

I scurry back toward the circulation desk, and there stands Stephanie Hannaham. I freeze, awestruck. She collects a stack of books from the librarian and turns. Stephanie sees me and smiles. My mind is a firework of flowers, and hers? Stephanie waves and leaves through the front door, as if she were any ordinary person.

On Monday, Stephanie wears a pink barrette in her hair, and I stare at it through my entire chem lab. Until:

"Miss Murphy, is Miss Hannaham's head more interesting than your assignment?"

The class erupts. I beg the floor to swallow me whole, but it does not oblige. My conjuring is limited to small objects. I cannot mutate linoleum. When the bell rings, I dodge around the back of the building, cutting across the field to hide under the bleachers until the coast is clear enough to walk home. As I duck under, I realize someone followed me. Stephanie. She must think I'm such a creep.

I slump to the ground. She sits next to me.

She. Sits. Next. To. Me.

I blurt an apology. She flashes that exploding smile and says, "Meg, it's okay. I think you're more interesting than the assignment too."

My eyes are so wide you can see them from space. Stephanie laughs, and my heart leaps to the roof of my mouth. She takes the pink barrette out of her hair and puts it in my hand. Managing only a hoarse croak, I ask her if she likes peonies. Then, before I can stop myself, I conjure the barrette into a glorious burst, a peony. She gasps. I hurry peony back to barrette, flustered and sputtering apologies.

She whispers, "Do it again."

We look at each other. I conjure the peony again. She looks at it. She looks at me. You can see her eyes from space. She takes a notebook out of her backpack and opens it to a drawing of a horse. She snaps her fingers, and the horse drawing leaps across the page. She murmurs, "Do you think we're cursed?"

I think about Sister Verena. I think about spitting toothpaste into the sink. I think about all the peonies in the universe and how they came to be. I look at Stephanie Hannaham sitting so close to me on the grass that we could share a root system. I reply and surprise myself by believing my own words, "How could anything so magnificent be a curse?"

I conjure a field of peonies on the page of Stephanie's notebook, and her horse gallops joyfully through. We blossom into a world they can no longer cut back.

Contributors:

Cover Artist:

Sarah Jane Walker was born in Jacksonville, Florida and attended the University of North Florida, where she received a BA in Psychology in 2017. She is both a practicing artist and an aspiring author. Sarah loves to convey an expression of mood through her art. She is also the proud mom of two precious children.

About *Tropical Forest*: Believe it or not, the piece, *Tropical Forest*, was painted in the middle of a harsh winter blizzard while spending time up in Canada with relatives. We were snowed-in, a feeling I wasn't used to, as I was originally born and raised in Florida. Freezing and missing the warmth of the sunshine state, I wanted to paint myself into a warmer place, willing myself to magically teleport through the power of art. I thought about painting Florida's swamp lands and its Spanish moss, but even that wasn't warm enough for me. So, I went even hotter, aiming for the majestic scenery of the tropical rainforest in South America, nearer to the equator. With this in mind, *Tropical Forest* is a mood piece intended to bring forth a positive emotion. It conveys the beauty of our planet, the creatures inhabiting it and, of course, the blissful sensation of simply being warm.

Levi Abadilla is a queer Filipino author who grew up in the Cebu province, and who enjoys all things weird and uncanny. Their work has been featured in *Stories After Dark, Hominum Journal,* and *Last Syllable.* More of their work can be found on leviabadilla.wordpress.com. When not writing, they can be found hanging out with their pets on their Instagram (@escapedscp) and Twitter (@nineaetharia).

Mike Bove is the author of four books of poetry, most recently *EYE* (Spuyten Duyvil, 2023). He serves as a 2024 Writer-in-Residence at Acadia National Park and is Associate Editor for *Hole in the Head Review.* Mike is Professor of English at Southern Maine Community College and lives with his family in Portland, Maine where he was born and raised. www.mikebove.com

Livy Burnett grew up in Lynchburg, Virginia. She has a BA in English from Harding University and an MFA in poetry from the University of Florida. Her work has placed in the Poets' Roundtable of Arkansas Jeannie Dolan writing contest and has been featured in *Cave Region Review.*

Allison Determan is an emerging writer from northern Massachusetts. She is currently pursuing her master's in biomedical engineering with a focus in neural engineering. Her previous work has been published multiple times in the *Long River Review*, University of Connecticut's student-run literary magazine

Anne Marie Fowler holds a Ph.D. in world literature in English and translation, an M.F.A. in poetry, an M.B.A. in Marketing, an M.B.A. in Management, and an M.A.in Organizational Leadership. Her creative work has been published nationally and internationally, and she is the editor of *Yellow as Turmeric, Fragrant as Cloves: A Contemporary Anthology of Asian American Women's Poetry*. She has also contributed to several encyclopedias on topics such as literature, sex workers, and online learning. She currently teaches composition, research, literature, creative writing, and mythology. Anne Marie's happy place is at the intersection of both of her creative loves: using her poetry in her artwork or as the genesis of an artistic exploration. In all creative work, she seeks to understand the magic of nature, the defining characteristics that make humans operate, and the connectivity of experience between and within cultures.

Isabel Gan is a Singaporean-American writer based in California who loves evocative imagery and the em dash. She is the founder and editor-in-chief of *Paper Cranes Literary*, and her work appears in *The Greyhound Journal, Fleeting Daze Magazine,* and *The Infinite Blues Review*. When not writing, she loves late-night musings, reading up on composers' biographies, and hot soup on rainy days.

Charity Gingerich's first full-length collection of poems, *After June*, won The Hopper poetry prize (Green Writers Press, 2019). Her chapbook, *Girl Escaping with Sky* was published by Dancing Girl Press (2014). Currently, she teaches ESL to international businesspersons and their families. Gingerich has received a poetry scholarship from the Sewanee Writer's Conference (2016) and a residency from the Vermont Studio Center (2019). Her work has appeared in journals such as *FIELD, the Kenyon Review, Arts & Letters, Ruminate*, and *Indiana Review*, among others. She is excited about going to France this summer with her choir to help celebrate the 80th anniversary of the liberation of Paris.

Emily Hoover is the author of the poetry chapbook, *My Mother as a Serrano Pepper* (*Zeitgeist Press,* 2023), and the forthcoming fiction micro-chapbook, *Sinners to the Back of the House: Stories About Women Who Leave (Bull City Press, 2025).* Her poetry, fiction, and reviews have been published by *Sundress Publications, The Citron Review, Cleaver Magazine, Necessary Fiction, Ploughshares blog, The Rupture,* and others. Emily's creative works have been nominated for the Pushcart Prize, *Best of the 'Net Anthology, Best Small Fictions Anthology,* and *Best Microfiction Anthology.* She lives in Las Vegas where she serves as Senior Lecturer of English and Creative Writing Coordinator at Nevada State University. She is also a Priority Editor at *Flash Fiction Magazine.* Find her on Instagram and X as @em1lywho.

Kaley Hutter writes from Virginia. Her work has previously appeared in *Meridian, Funicular Magazine, Little Patuxent Review,* and elsewhere. Kaley also teaches collegiate composition, serves as an editor for the literary magazine *LAMP*, and works to create and pursue joy.

Alexis Jaimes, a proud son of Mexican immigrants, resides in Santa Ana, CA. He recently published his first chapbook through Bottlecap Press, "*Corazón Coalesced.*" Jaimes weaves together the tender and the tumultuous, offering readers a journey through the struggles and beauty found in exploring love, identity, and heritage. His works have also been previously featured in *Polemical Zine, Alegría Magazine, Loud Coffee Press, San Diego Poetry Annual, Moon Tide Press, ¡Pa'lante!* and *MUSE Literary Journal.* He has also been showcased at the acclaimed Fullerton Museum Center. Alexis obtained his BA in English from California State University, Long Beach, and later pursued an MS and teaching credential from California State University, Fullerton, to become a bilingual elementary teacher. Through his writing, Alexis strives to empower and uplift his community, using words as a vehicle for positive change. You can follow him on IG at @alexjaimes182.

Sarah Rachael Johnnes was raised near New York City and currently resides in the Pacific Northwest. As an emerging poet, Sarah applies her photographic eye bringing visual sensibilities to her poetry. She is focused on capturing what is not typically seen, finding connection, beauty, and humor in common everyday moments—or moments that reflect decay or, pain and taboo subjects. Her work has appeared online: *Cathexis Northwest, Fauxmoir Literary Journal, RavensPerch, Red Ogre Review*, and *Black Fox Literary Magazine*. Another one will be in the winter edition of the Westchester Review. Sarah is working on a collection of poems.

Sarah Kersey earned her MFA in poetry from Eastern Washington University in 2022. Her work has been published or is upcoming in *Poet Lore, Atlanta Review, Hunger Mountain*, and more. She was a finalist in *Atlanta Review's* 2022 International Poetry Contest, as well as a finalist in *Sunspot Literary Journal's* 2022 Geminga contest. She currently teaches English at Gonzaga University and North Idaho College.

Ela Kini is a student based in New York. She is a YoungArts winner and Scholastic Art & Writing Awards gold medalist. Her work appears in *Palette Poetry, Cargoes,* and *Apricity*, as well as elsewhere. She loves lattes.

Angela Kirby resides in Pennsylvania, where she spends her time writing and practicing the art of paper quilling. Her short story "Memories in the Rearview" was awarded Honorable Mention in the 91st Annual Writer's Digest Writing Competition for 2022.

Zelime Lewis is a semi-nomadic writer currently based in the UK. She earned an MFA in Writing from Sarah Lawrence College and an undergraduate degree in English Literature from the University of St. Andrews. At Sarah Lawrence College she was a fiction Editor for the MFA-run journal, *Lumina*. Originally from a tiny mountain town in Colorado, she gravitates towards writing about place and isolation. When she's not writing, she is an amateur potter and enjoys drinking pretentious espresso drinks out of her own handmade mugs.

Carolina Mata is a queer Xicana writer, editor, and bruja from the Coachella Valley. Her MFA comes from CSU, Fresno where she served as Senior Editor for *The Normal School*. Her work can be found in *The San Joaquin Review, The Painted Cave, the Wild Blue Zine, Psychopomp Magazine*, and elsewhere. She's currently Social Media Co-Director and a flash reader for *Split Lip Magazine*. Connect with her @bigsisartwitch (X).

S Maxfield is a genderqueer, bi+, and disabled writer with roots in dance and theater. Maxfield's published fiction includes a short story featured in *We Mostly Come Out at Night: 15 Queer Tales of Monsters, Angels & Other Creatures* (Running Press, 2024) and a flash fiction story in *Just YA*, an open-license anthology for educators forthcoming from Oklahoma State University (OpenOK State, 2024). Maxfield's flash fiction has also been published by *Voyage YA/Uncharted* and *WinC Magazine*, and their debut comics collection *Assorted Sweets* sold out twice at the legendary NYC comics shop Forbidden Planet, after successfully funding through Kickstarter. Maxfield grew up in a log cabin, but has spent the past two decades in NYC, where s/he lives with their family and imaginary cat Dragon. Find out more at: linktr.ee/essmaxfield.

Eden Mecham is the pen name of a writer and editor living in rural Vermont. She received her MFA from the University of Massachusetts, and she's also worked as a Grub Street instructor in Boston. Her work has been published in various literary journals and magazines.

Devon Neal (he/him) is a Kentucky-based poet whose work has appeared in many publications, including *HAD, Stanchion, Livina Press, The Storms,* and *The Bombay Lit Mag*, and has been nominated for Best of the Net. He currently lives in Bardstown, KY with his wife and three children.

Winslow Schmelling is a writer and teacher from the Sonoran Desert. As an ex-professional pizza maker and current content marketer, she feels lucky to be a part of the creative community in the desert where she grew up. Her creative work appears in *LitHub, Peatsmoke Journal, Heavy Feather Review, Wild Roof Journal* and elsewhere. She earned her MFA in fiction from Arizona State University. Find her at winslowschmelling.com

Audrey Towns, a literature and composition instructor in the heart of Fort Worth, Texas, dismantles the nature/culture binary in her prose and verse. She has published, or is forthcoming, in *Driftwood Press Anthology, Spellbinder Quarterly Literary and Arts Magazine, The Amphibian Literary and Arts Journal*, and *Willawaw Journal*, among others.

Alexa Vallejo is a transfemme, Filipina American writer and musician living in West Philadelphia. Her work has appeared in *swamp pink, TriQuarterly, The Rumpus, Guernica*, and the *Asian American Literary Review*, among others. She has been nominated for a Best of the Net Award and twice for a Pushcart Prize. She performs music under the name Sasha V.

Deanna Whitlow is an MFA candidate in Fiction at Columbia College Chicago. She is the Editorial Assistant for *Allium: A Journal of Poetry and Prose* as well as the founder and Editor-in-chief of *Same Faces Collective*. Her work can be found in *Mulberry Literary, Hair Trigger, Identity Theory*, and others.

Tyler Wilson is a songwriter and poet living in Brooklyn, NY.

Special shoutout to the longlisters of our contests!

Fairy Tale Remix (BFLM Winter Prize) Longlist:

Katelin Garner for "The Hunger and the Wolf Machine"

Christine Boyer for "Under the Skin"

Kevin Sandefur for "The Magic Notebook"

Terri Mullholland for "A Fairy-Tale Romance"

Devony Hof for "Seven Pigeons"

Phoebe Barr for "Cinder and Fire"

Gabrielle Langley for "Instagram Posts for My Father"

Kay Ben-Avraham for "The Teind of Tam Lin"

Rose Engelfried for "Bear Skin"

Jeff Stumpo for "The Shoemaker and the Elves"

Finch Greene for "when i say *someday my prince will come…*"

Miriam Fietz for "Bluebeard's Closet [unboxed]"

Brigette Stevenson for "Liesel and the Black Woods"

Bonnie Markowski for "Fairy Fall"

Montage of Misfortunes (Spring Fox Tales) Longlist:

Carla Schick for "Reasons for Surviving"

Bonnie Shao for "an airbag deploys in less than 1/20th of a second"

Emily Hoover for "Lines Composed on the Morning After You Left Me," and "The Match We Lit"

Emillia Nunn for "Trying to Love a Tree in August"

Lynne Schmidt for "Windshield Glass"

Emily Harris for "la mia luna, before"

Morgan Rose-Marie for "He Knows: The Dog Dies in This One"

Suzette Bishop for "Sparkling Ice Plains"

Harrison Hamm for "Eulogy for the Pomegranate"

We love seeing photos of readers enjoying *Black Fox*! Please help us spread the word by posting about *Black Fox* on your social accounts. Be sure to tag us in your posts!

Thank you for reading! Stay in touch:

www.blackfoxlitmag.com
Website

www.facebook.com/blackfoxlit
Facebook

@blackfoxlit
Twitter & Instagram

www.blackfoxlitmag.com/contact/
Newsletter

Check out some of our previous issues in the *Black Fox* Shop!

blackfoxlitmag.com/shop

Resources for Writers from BFLM Editor Racquel Henry's Writer's Atelier:

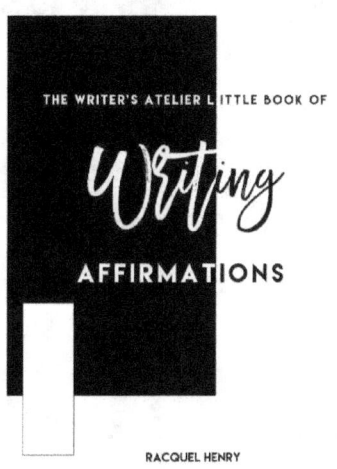

The Writer's Atelier Little Book of Writing Affirmations

The Write Gym Workbook by Racquel Henry

Join Racquel's free online community for writers:

writersatelier.mn.co

www.ingramcontent.com/pod-product-compliance
Lightning Source LLC
Chambersburg PA
CBHW060421260626
47161CB00005B/1721